BODILESS

Amber King

ISBN: 9781980236955

Printed by Amazon Kindle Self-Publishing., in the United States of America.

First printing edition 2018.
www.hyperfury.com

~To my wonderful mother and grandmother, thank you for always being there and inspiring me with your wisdom and strength. To my love, thank you for believing in my pipe dreams and encouraging me to never give up. To my band mates, Hyper Fury, thank you guys for taking a chance on me. Being in this band has been the best time of my life and I'm proud to be a part of it. No matter where our music takes us, I'm happy to know that we created something special~

Dedication

Table of Contents

1 5

2.. 19

3 32

4.. 44

5 58

6.. 64

7 73

8.. 89

9.. 98

10 111

11 122

12 138

13.. 151

14 161

15.. 169

16.. 188

17.. 198

18.. 210

19 217

20 230

21 245

22.. 251

23.. 264

24 271

1

I woke up from death feeling utterly weak. The light is overpowering, and I quickly cover my eyes. My head feels like it weighs a ton, and my lower body feels completely numb. I slowly open my eyes again, and after a minute of adjusting, my vision comes back to me. I observe my hands and arms, and to my surprise, they look and feel exactly as I remember.

I wiggle my hands and toes to make sure that they are working properly, and I am relieved to find that they are. I stretch my limbs, popping multiple joints throughout my body, then attempt to stand. I succeed and take my first steps in what feels like an eternity. I am...alive. I'm alive-ish? I can't believe it.

The small feeling of gratitude quickly vanishes as I observe my surroundings.

None of this makes sense. I died on my living room floor; if I were alive, then that's where I would be. That or the hospital. I look around to get a feel of the place. There are spots of grass among what appears to be an endless dirt landscape. There are mountains painted with red erosion as far as the eye can see. I discover that I'm located on top of a smaller mountain as I notice that I'm about 100 feet from the edge. I look up at the sky and see only gray clouds stretching across like a withered quilt.

Something is peculiar about the clouds. Not that it looks ominous—which it does—but it's something else. The clouds don't appear to be moving anywhere. On the contrary, the wind is blustery, and I hear thunder in the background. None of this makes sense. Where am I? Is this my hell? Oh, no... This may be my hell. I look down and notice that I'm still wearing my white nightgown and matching flip-flops—my death clothes.

I decide to start screaming for help. If I can find people, I can find answers. I really hope so. This is all a shock to my system, and I'm overwhelmed with confusion. I turn around so my back is against the windstorm. As I do, a flash of lightning touches the sky, followed by a boisterous thunder clap.

I begin to hyperventilate. I fall to my knees, trying hard to breathe, but the wind pressure is too heavy. Dirt begins to mix with the air, creating little dirt vortexes. I can only breathe dirt-filled air, and my lungs are slowly collapsing. I feel like I'm dying all over again. I fall face-first onto the ground ready to meet my maker...once more. I roll over onto my back, coughing and wheezing. I look over and see the dirt vortex grow larger until it forms a fucking tornado! I close my eyes and slowly turn away, anticipating the powerful force to sweep me away like a plastic bag. I unexpectedly feel heat radiating against my face, and it's the first warm feeling I've had since I died.

I open my eyes and see a small, round, beautiful, white light about the size of a baseball. I jump, completely startled by it flying around the air in a zig-zag motion, like a bumblebee. I realize that this light is trying to get my attention. It's trying to tell me something. Maybe it wants me to follow it and lead me to safety!

I stand as quickly as I can and begin running after this light. I notice that the wind is rising with each passing second. I turn around and realize that the tornado has gotten too close for comfort. Panic overflows in me, and adrenaline follows shortly after. Out of impulse, I begin running at the light, full speed. The only thing in existence at this point is me, this light, and the tornado close behind. I'm running, getting closer and closer, and without thinking, I reach out in attempt to grab it.

I feel nothing but air, and the next thing I know, I'm slipping from solid ground. I was so transfixed by the light, that I didn't notice myself running off a damn cliff! I tumble for what feels like forever, hitting pebbles and twigs along the way. I'm twisting and turning, feeling helpless and disposable. I wish this nightmare would end. I soon get my wish when my head slams into a rock, knocking me unconscious.

I slowly begin to regain consciousness, and I feel something on my face. I open my eyes to find myself lying on the ground with that ball of light hovering over me. I quickly rise, feeling a sudden adrenaline rush throughout my body. I stare at this light, examining and trying to understand it. It soon becomes clear that it is studying me too. It moves around like a being, but I'm sensing a peaceful vibe from it.

"Thank you for saving me. I don't know where I am or what you are, but thank you," I say.

The light fumbles around, flying closer. As I reach out to touch it, I finally get a clear look at it. It resembles an inverted triangle with a circle in the center, which is a symbol for something, I'm sure. Without realization, I ask, "What are you?" The light starts flying around me. I find myself trying to follow its every move. I'm spinning around trying to keep up, but it's moving too fast for me. Suddenly, it takes off, leaving me behind.

"Hey!" I exclaim. I begin running after it, trying to keep it in my line of vision. I'm running as fast as I can, but it seems that the faster I run, the farther it goes. Where is it going? Is it trying to lead me somewhere? My mind is riddled with questions, but my main concern right now is tracking this light. Right now, it's my only guide in this chaotic world.

* * *

"Hey, come back! Wait!" I keep running, unaware of my surroundings. The light is getting brighter, which means I'm getting closer. As soon as I begin to pick up speed, I crash into someone. I fall onto the ground, landing on top of this person. I'm suddenly elated. The light led me to another person! I remove myself from the ground, and before I speak, I look at this man.

He is an old, frail-looking man with gray skin. From head to toe, even his clothes are gray, as if he is rotting all over. It seems as if he rolled in a pile of ash, and didn't bother to wash it off. I hold my hand out to help him up, but he just stares at me.

His eyes are cold, lifeless, and black. I look a little closer and see that his irises are missing; only pupils remain in his empty eyes. I turn around in haste only to witness a herd of gray-colored people walking through. I realize that I am standing in the center of a dirt road full of lifeless people, mindlessly staggering around like zombies. I turn back around to face the old man, but he isn't there.

Fear begins crawling down my spine as I take all this in. How did these people get like this? Are they still conscious? Do they still feel anything? Will I become one of these people? I decide to see if I can talk to one of them. Maybe someone is still in touch with their humanity, though that's highly doubtful.

I run toward a man in a torn-up police uniform that's gray like the rest. I try to get his attention. "Sir, excuse me. Can you hear me?" He walks past me like I'm not even there. I try someone else, but I get the same results. I keep running, bumping into people, trying to get someone to hear me. Nothing happens. I run in the opposite direction of everyone else, yelling, tapping shoulders, and bumping into them, but I get no response. Everyone just keeps walking in silence. One guy is prancing in a straight line like a lunatic, heading in the same direction as everyone else. I realize that this isn't a safe place for me to be.

As I turn around to leave, I'm surprised by a tall man standing very close to me. He's staring at me with a cold-hearted grin, matching his black eyes. He is pitch-black from head to toe, standing out from everyone around us. Overwhelming fear begins to take control of me, and I feel my whole body shaking. I inhale deeply as I begin to slowly back away from him.

As I'm backing away, I bump into a hard chest. I turn around to find a man with flesh that resembled a rotting corpse. He has flaky, gray skin that shrivel like dead leaves and lips that have been ripped off, exposing his decaying teeth and gum line. He is wearing a tattered pilot suit, with his collar and arms ripped apart and a bullet hole under his chin. Instead of blood, a tar-like substance oozes out of his mangled chin. He has the same black eyes, except his are filled with fury.

I'm left speechless, paralyzed with fear. The more I keep searching for help, the more I keep finding trouble. The pilot pushes me, and I land in the other guy's arms. The other man pushes me back into the pilot.

I yell, "Stop it!" but it only eggs them on. I'm pushed again into the other guy, and out of reflex, I hit him as hard as I can. He stumbles a bit, but quickly regains his composure. He looks at me, and I watch his eyes turn from black to red. I try to run, but the pilot grabs me and forces me to kneel.

I begin to panic. The only thing I can do is yell, in my moment of terror. I scream for help, hoping someone will hear me. Where is that damn light? Can't it see that I need help? The light led me here; where is it now?

The man gets closer, carrying a maniacal grin on his face. I'm squirming around, trying to release myself from the pilot's grip, but my efforts go nowhere. I'm still screaming for help, but all I see are these damn zombies stumbling to nowhere. I stop screaming, realizing that I'm beating on a dead horse while the blind continues to lead the blind.

The pilot pulls my hair, yanking my head back, and I can hear chattering teeth. I close my eyes, ready to be stabbed or eaten or whatever these vile creatures do. I say creatures because whatever humanity they had must have been gone for a long time. Suddenly, I feel cold water splashing my face. I start coughing up the water that invaded my throat. I'm released from the pilot's hands, and I fall to the ground, still wheezing. I hear the pilot belt out a loud shriek, and I open my eyes to see a man.

He's human like me, wearing a fire fighter uniform and holding a primitive clay bowl. The other creature hisses at the fireman. The fireman throws the water onto him, causing the monster to squeal in pain. The creatures run away, rejoining the herd of the dead.

I pick myself up from the ground and dust myself off. The man drops the bowl and runs over to me. "Are you okay? That was pretty close; they almost got you."

I'm still in the process of calming myself down, but when I hear his voice—a human voice—I feel immediate relief. Without thinking, I grab him and hug him tighter than I've ever hugged anyone. Well, almost anyone... I feel him softly pat me on the back.

He speaks again. "It's okay. You're safe now. What's your name? What do you remember?" His tone is slightly deep but placid. I release him from the hug, slightly embarrassed, and I take a good look at him for the first time.

He looks like he is in his mid-twenties, over six feet tall, with short brown hair, blue eyes, and a muscular build. He is the quintessential all-American boy, which makes me wonder why he is here in the first place. What happened to him? I'm stuck with questions, but at least I'm not alone anymore.

I answer his question after a moment. "My name is Cadence. I just woke up in this place. I woke up on the mountain range, and I...managed to get to lower ground. This ball of light led me here, then I lost it, and now—"

"Whoa. Rewind that for me," he interjects.

"I said I just woke up in this place and—"

He interjects again, "No, not that—about the ball of light."

I look at him, exasperated. "Yes, a ball of light helped me get off that mountain and led me here. It was helping me, and then it just flew off. We have to find the light; I think it can lead us away from this place and maybe find some peace...or something. Hell, maybe even bring us back to life." The man starts laughing, like what I said is the best joke he's ever heard. Does he not realize that I'm as serious as my suicide? I'm failing to find the humor in all of this.

"Hey, I'm serious. It may be our way out."

He gives me a look of pity, and I know that he's about to drop a bomb on me. "Cadence, look, you just got here. You've been through a lot already, and I understand that you don't know what the hell is going on, so I feel obligated to tell you. We are stuck in the void."

In confusion, I ask, "What does that mean, 'void?' Is this like purgatory or something?"

"All I know about this place is that suicidal people come here and stay until one day, their human body disappears. Those people walking along the road are dead inside. No humanity left inside, and one day, they will fade away and cease to exist. I guess that's why a lot of roamers call this place "the void."

I ask him, "So what were those things that attacked me?"

"We call them the dark ones, but there is no official name for them, we don't think. From what I know, they were vile, dysfunctional people in their lifetime. They brought those qualities here, and let the darkness overcome them. They like inflicting pain on others, and they get off on fear. You can't be afraid of them if you see one. They will want to eat your soul even more."

"Wait, they were after my soul?!"

"Yes, it's the only way they can stay in the void. They are dangerous. Don't go anywhere by yourself without water. Water helps to keep us human longer, and I guess that's why it hurts them so much."

Wow. I can't believe I almost had my soul eaten by those monsters. I am stuck here in this hell without fire with only myself to blame. What did I just get myself into?

"My name is Phoenix. I'm not sure how long I've been here, but it feels like an eternity. I can't remember the year I died anymore. The longer you stay here, the more you start to lose yourself. It happens to everyone."

I start shaking my head profusely. That doesn't make sense to me. "No, I don't believe that. Think about it. Why else would we be here other than to reflect?"

Phoenix looks at me perplexed. "You think this is a place of reflection?"

"You think this is a place of punishment?" I ask.

"Yeah, I do," says Phoenix. "Cadence, you haven't been here as long as I have. I've witnessed the horrors of this place and what it does to people."

I scan the area to become more aware of my surroundings. It's a habit I should get used to, I suppose. "If we were here to be punished, then we would be...well...getting punished. I almost suffocated and got sucked inside a tornado. Then I stumbled off the mountaintop to almost have my soul eaten. Now I'm here with you. Even after all of that, I still can't believe that this is a place of punishment. If it was, then why aren't we being burnt to a crisp or being tortured? Why did it lead me to you?"

"Sounds like you have been punished to me, Cadence?" Phoenix replies.

I'm not sure if that was meant to be a joke, but I can't help but laugh because he kind of got me there. I admit that this ordeal has been rough, and maybe I would see his perspective if I didn't come across that being made of light. That being is our way out; I know it. It led me here to people—a bumpy journey, but I got here. I know it. I just do.

I look him in the eyes and speak. "I don't know. I can't explain it. I felt something when I saw that light, and I knew that I had to follow it, and eventually, it led me here to you. After everything we've seen, why is it so hard to believe in a ball of light?"

"You're asking me to believe in hope. There was once a crazy guy here who thought he saw a light just like you described. He thought he was saved, and you know what happened to him? He disappeared like the rest. Look, we can continue this conversation later. You can join our group. We have shelter. We don't eat food in the void, but we have plenty of water." I nod at his accommodations, and he puts his hand on my shoulder. "You should get some rest; you had it rough so far." He guides his hand along my back, propelling me in front of him.

We are both in shock when we see the ball of light levitating in front of us. Phoenix's chiseled jaw nearly drops to the ground. I feel his hand drop from my back, and he just stands there, incapable of moving.

I walk closer to the light, grateful to see it in this moment. "Hey, you. I've been looking all over for you. Is there any way you can communicate?"

The light flies around in a zig-zag motion again. I look over to Phoenix, and he still hasn't moved. I turn back to the light, and it takes off again. "Hey, wait!" I yell, running after it. I turn around and see Phoenix still standing there, frozen. I run back to him and grab his hand. "Come on! We have to catch up to it!"

We both begin running after it. We keep running, jumping over rocks, and running against the unsettling wind. We keep moving, and I suddenly feel mist brush against my face and hear sounds of flowing water. I yell to Phoenix, "You hear that? It sounds like there's a river up ahead!"

He replies, "Yeah, I know! That's where my group and I camp out!"

"How convenient!" I yell, relieved that I've finally found a haven.

2

I ask Phoenix, "So, are you a believer now?"

He smiles for the first time. His perfectly aligned smile is slightly crooked but charming with his crinkled dimples. He's so handsome when he's happy.

He replies, "Well, seeing is believing, isn't it?"

We keep running, and I notice his camp about half a mile away. We lost track of the light, unfortunately. Phoenix and I stop running, both panting and trying to catch our breath.

"I think we lost it," Phoenix says as he bends over to rest his hands on his knees.

I reply, "Yeah. I could use some water right about now. I'm feeling a little weak."

We walk over to his camp, which is just a couple of mud huts that stands a few yards from the free-flowing river. I have never seen water like this before. The color is violet, and it sparkles as if there are specks of crystals mixed inside. The current flows smooth and free without a single pollutant. It looks flawless.

We soon arrive to Phoenix's camp, where I see two men writing something on the ground with sticks. One is a tall, slim, white man with dark hair and glasses. Judging off his looks, he must have been in his late twenties to early thirties when he died. He's dressed in khaki pants with a light blue dress shirt and black Converse shoes. Black, horn-rimmed glasses cover his deep, sea-green eyes, and his hair is perfectly combed to the right side of his face. He seems like the quintessential nerd. We walk a few more feet before I finally notice the noose around his neck. I think I can guess how he got here.

The other guy is a black man, which, for some reason, consoles me that there is another person of color here. He's facing away from me, so I can't get a good look at him. I can hear his voice the closer I get, though. I notice that his accent has a southern drawl. I also notice his attire: a green- and brown-striped polo shirt with khaki pants and athletic shoes.

I finally get close enough to see what they're writing. I realize that they are playing hangman, of all games. Only a masochist would play a game that reminds him of how he died. Maybe it's his way of making lemonade out of lemons; it's not like I have any room to judge.

I begin observing the game, trying to calculate how soon it would end. The hangman is almost fully formed, with only the legs missing. There are seven letters filled in: D E A _ _ H S _ A R.

The black guy speaks. "I'm going to say the letter...S."

"No, you already used S. One more and you get hanged, just like the rest of us are anyway. Why are we playing this again?"

The black guy shrugs his shoulders and answers, "I don't know. You suggested it. We should pick a different game. I hate hangman, and you pick shitty words."

The guy with the glasses gives him a crooked smile and says, "Hey, that's not very civil. Besides, the answer is obvious; you're just not thinking about it. But if you're giving up, I may as well tell you."

I feel like it's a good time to interject, so I speak. "The word is DEATH STAR."

The men turn around in haste, confirming their unawareness of our presence. Phoenix appears by my side and says, "Hey, guys. This is Cadence. She's going to be joining our...group. Cadence," Phoenix points to the black guy, "that is Craig, the other one is Max. Guys, say hello."

The nerdy guy who I now know to be Max offers me a handshake and a genuine smile. I return a firm handshake along with my best "it's nice to meet you" smile. Max says, "Kudos for the death star answer. It's nice to see that even in the afterlife, *Star Wars* still lives on. "

I give him a brief chuckle to be friendly, but I did find that comment kinda funny. There is a brief silence after the greeting. I break it by saying, "Max, it's nice to meet you. Have you been here long?"

"Well, that's a hard question to answer. Does it feel like we've been here for ions? Yes. We can't keep up with time in this realm because time is kind of bullshit. All our lives wasted on worrying about time, an illusion humanity has deemed relative. We don't know how long we've been here, and neither will you."

I take in his words, studying his tone. He wasn't angry or yelling or even sad, for that matter. The only thing I heard was a broken man who just didn't care anymore. I look over to Craig, and see that he is just sitting on the ground cross-legged, drawing patterns in the dirt. I notice a small hut made of a mixture of mud and rocks. The foundation appears to be strong and well put together. I wonder if they found this place or if they settled here.

I feel a hand on my shoulder, and I look over to find Phoenix attached to it. He squeezes my shoulder slightly, and I feel safe. I realize that he isn't just a dead guy in a firefighter suit; he sincerely wants to provide safety for his group, and I guess for me too.

We have been through a lot already, but this is only the beginning. Phoenix walks over to a pile of sticks and split logs and grabs an armful. He drops it in the fire pit that I am just realizing exists right in the middle of camp, which is just a hole, maybe a foot deep. He quickly sparks a fire, and soon, the flames start to blow fiercely against the wind. We all silently sit in a circle around the fire.

Max offers me a shriveled orchid leaf containing a small amount of violet water, and I gratefully accept. The water is bubbly, but the mist escaping the leaf makes my skin tingle. That sensation alone takes me back to the days when I was a carefree child running through neighbors' water sprinklers during hot seasons.

I take my first gulp of this violet water, and for the first time since I've arrived here, I feel revitalized.

The water is sweet and bubbly like a carbonated drink, but goes down smoother. I take another gulp, savoring the taste as I swallow this unique water. Why couldn't we have had this on Earth? I've seen and tasted spring water, but this doesn't compare. I look up to see

Phoenix staring at me, giggling slightly. Max joins in on the giggling.

"That water is divine, isn't it? If I only had that water to grow my weed. Damn, I wouldn't even be here." Max says.

"You smoked weed?" I ask, surprised by his revelation.

Max gives me that perplexed look you give when someone asks you a stupid question. He replies, "Honey, you would lose your jaw if you knew the things I've done."

I let out a laugh at his words and logic. I give an awkward response, saying, "Well, I like my jaw where it is. Maybe we should spill our sins another day."

Max holds his leaf in the air, giving a silent toast, before taking another sip. That's when I'm reminded of that white light. Since we are all here, I figured now would be a good time to bring it up.

I nudge Phoenix's shoulder to get his attention and say, "So, I was thinking about telling them about the being of light we saw earlier. What do you think about that?"

Phoenix tilts his head with uncertainty. "Well, we can. I can't promise they will believe us."

His answer frustrates me more than it should. "Well, whether they believe us or not, I'm following the light, regardless. We both know it's real, and I bet the remainder of my existence that it will help us find our way out of here."

Phoenix seems a little shaken by what I just said. He's just coming to the realization of how serious I am, and he's right. I will not let this go. If there's a way out of here, I'm not missing my stop, and I don't want them to miss theirs either.

Phoenix takes a deep breath. "Guys, we need to let you in on a little something. I—"

He gets interrupted by a woman crawling out of the hut. She quietly walks over and sits between me and Max. It is then that I begin to slowly observe her.

She looks so...plastic—dysmorphic, even. She has an orange tan, her skin has a rubberlike texture, her forehead sits very low on her face, and her lips look like they are one injection away from bursting like a balloon. She also has breasts the size of soccer balls that barely fit in her dress. The surgeon who botched her up like that should put a bullet in his brain and come directly here to apologize to her.

Even her wardrobe is peculiar: a beautiful, silk, white wedding dress with blood spatter invading the fabric's perfection. I notice that her bridal veil is moved away from her face, and then I see her eyes. Her vibrant, baby blue, almond-shaped eyes tell a story of fear and sadness. She looks down, obviously uncomfortable with my staring. I look away, realizing how rude my behavior is.

Phoenix speaks. "Hey, sorry I forgot to introduce you two. Cadence, this is Daphne. Daphne, Cadence."

"It's nice to meet you, Daphne." I reach for her hand, but she turns the other way.

Phoenix leans over and whispers, "She doesn't speak. She hasn't said a single word since we found her here, except for her name. She means well and isn't dangerous, she just doesn't talk very much."

I nod, understanding the circumstances. We sit silently by the fire, trying to ignore the gusty wind behind us. It's hard to wrap my mind around the fact that I'm dead, surrounded by dead strangers, and the only hope I have to cling on so far is this ball of light.

After a while, I break the silence by asking Phoenix, "So what's with the firefighter outfit? Were you a firefighter or male stripper?" Everyone laughs except Daphne, but she did smile a little.

Phoenix lets out an awkward sigh, scratching his head. "No, I was not a stripper, so sorry to disappoint. I was a firefighter. I dedicated my life to it. So, I thought it made sense to wear it when I...you know...killed myself."

My heart drops as he speaks those words. His death clothes. He took the time to think about what he was going to wear and how he was going to go out. I couldn't even do that. I was just impulsive and didn't want to feel the pain anymore. I don't know what that makes me or him. I guess we're all just fucked up.

Once again, here I am being intrusive. I'm usually not this way; at least I don't think I am. I should leave the subject alone.

"I'm sure you were great at it. Hey, you saved me." I say, trying to lighten the mood.

He looks at me and nods politely. We grow silent again, embracing the sounds of the fire crackling and the river flowing behind us. It feels good to just sit here in front of a fire. Fire was always my favorite element; a combustion of passionate, rebellious energy that's unforgivingly captivating. I feel myself drifting into sleep, surrendering to this temporary escape from reality.

* * *

"WAKE UP!!!!!"

I'm suddenly jolted awake. I look around and see Max and Craig in a defensive position holding large, wooden sticks, ready to strike. I jump up from the ground and run over to Daphne, who has her hands covering her face.

"The dark ones are here. A lot of them. We must keep them away. Stay behind the fire!" Max yells.

I see the dark ones coming. As in a fuck-ton of them. We can't fight them all off. There're too many. They begin to form a circle around us to trap us.

Phoenix yells, "Guys, they are surrounding us, trying to block us in! We have to go now before it's too late!"

Max interjects, "No, are you crazy? We leave the fire, they get us!"

Phoenix replies, "We stay here, they fucking get us, man!"

Max yells, "Well where do you suggest we go?"

An idea pops into my head, and I yell, "The river, guys! They can't get us there. We can swim somewhere safe."

Max turns to me and says, "Yeah, that can't be safe."

"Do you have any better ideas?" I ask harshly, trying to decide something so we don't die.

Max looks to me, then the dark ones. He sees Craig running toward the water, and yells, "Okay, let's just go now!"

Just as Max turns around to run, one of the dark ones grabs the end of Max's noose, yanking him toward them.

"No!" I shout. I begin to run after him, but stop myself because they were already surrounding him. They swarm around him until the sight of his body disappears and is replaced by the sound of his screams.

Phoenix, Daphne, and I run toward the river with the dark ones close behind. We run until the shallow end turns into the deep end, and then we swim until the dark ones are far in the distance. We stop swimming and begin to float, physically tired but alert. I feel a rain drop fall on my face. I look up and see the ball of light flying above.

"Hey, guys, look up; there's the light again!" I exclaim in jubilation.

By the time everyone looks up, it's gone. My hope shatters once again. How am I supposed to explain this to them?

Craig speaks. "There's nothing there but clouds. You've been seeing a ball of light?" I look at him strangely, realizing that he's already familiar with it.

I reply, "Yes, I have been, and it's what helped me find you guys. I think it's trying to help us get out of here."

Craig interjects. "Oh, great. How many times are people going to fall for that? Look, it's just in your mind. It's not real. It's just something people make up, so they can have a false sense of hope."

"Do you hear yourself? How is it that a group of random people claim to have witnessed the same thing?" I ask.

Phoenix joins in. "She's right. I saw it too, not long after I found Cadence."

Craig scoffs. "Look, you may like her and want to get in her pants, but that doesn't make her right. Sorry. Besides, I doubt sex is possible in this place, so give it up."

Where does he get off?

Before I could say anything, Phoenix interjects. "Seems to me you're projecting your feelings onto me. Is that why you killed yourself? Is it because girls like her never gave you the time of day? Don't talk like you know the game if you've never managed to score?"

Craig yells, "Fuck you! You don't know shit about me! Don't test me!"

"Or what? You'll kill me?" Phoenix asks, condescendingly.

"Can we please get back to important issues like, I don't know, trying to get out of this fucking river?!" I yell at them, frustrated at their petty arguing.

The ball of light appears right in front of us, flying in a downward spiral. It dives into the water, causing it to light up around us. Suddenly, the river begins to spin like a whirlpool. We're all spinning and sinking. I try to scream, but before I know it, I'm underwater, spinning along with everyone else. As I'm spinning, I see the ball of light right in front of me. I try to reach for it, but darkness falls around me, and I quickly surrender to it.

3

I awaken, standing next to everyone in an apartment bedroom. I feel completely bedazzled. I have no idea what is going on. We are all completely dry like we had never touched water. I look toward Daphne, and she is looking down at her feet. Phoenix is standing near the corner of the room, arms crossed, looking at everyone else. I turn to Craig and he has a blank expression on his face. It dawns on me that this place is familiar to him. He knows this place. Maybe this was his place. Where have we landed ourselves?

Craig walks around the room, studying it. He sees a Batman poster on the wall and tries to touch it. Some sort of invisible barrier appears, causing Craig to yank his hand away.

This is his memory—a day in his life.

We are inside his life right now. Are we all going to experience this? Am I next? My breathing begins racing, realizing the gravity of our situation. This could be good, right? We are out of the void and inside of

Craig's memories. This has got to be a step toward the real afterlife—somewhere positive. It must, right?

Craig finally breaks the silence. "How is this possible? This is where I lived, and it looks just how I left it. I can't explain why, but I feel really uncomfortable being here."

Suddenly, a different "Craig" walks into the bedroom. He shuts the door and sits on the end of his bed. We all look at "our" Craig in utter confusion. He stands motionless, still as a statue, with eyes full of tears.

I ask, "What's going on, Craig?"

He doesn't respond. His eyes are drawn to his doppelganger. The other Craig grabs the remote from the bed and turns the radio onto an r&b station. His face is emotionless, and he seems completely checked out. He then reaches under the bed and grabs a black shoe box. My heart sinks into my stomach. This isn't what I think it is. I look over to our Craig, who is cringing at the scene unfolding before us. Before I ponder the many things that could be in the box, I hear a gunshot.

We all scream in terror, having just witnessed Craig's suicide. His brain is spread across his bedpost. His lifeless body lying there on the bed with his finger still latched on the trigger.

Our Craig snaps out of his trance. "What the fuck is this? Why am I here seeing this? This makes no sense!" He turns to me. "You. You brought us here. Tell me what is going on now!"

I'm in utter disbelief. This is not what I had in mind about moving on. I speak. "I don't know what's going on. I was just trying to get us away from the dark ones. I didn't know it would bring us here. To this."

Craig takes a deep breath before continuing his rant. "Okay, well get us out of here, then. Find that crystal ball or whatever it is, and make it guide us the hell out of here."

Phoenix suddenly interjects. "Actually, I think we are right where we are supposed to be." We all turn toward Phoenix in surprise.

Craig gives a condescending laugh before replying, "You wouldn't be saying that if you just witnessed your death."

Phoenix interjects, "No. Think about it, guys. We have been stuck in that void since we died. I think the fact that we're not there anymore is a step forward. This also explains why people disappear after claiming they had seen it."

Craig begins pacing nervously, and it seems like he's slowly beginning to spiral out of control. He angrily walks right up to Phoenix's face, pointing to his dead body, and says, "Does my death seem like a fucking work in progress to you?"

Phoenix takes a step back. "You need to calm down. Fighting will not get us anywhere. Our lives are literally staring us in the face. We can either choose to look away and die, or we can face it."

"Together," I say, unsure if I mean that as a question or a statement.

Phoenix looks at me. "Yeah, we can all get through this, maybe find some peace, and move on to something else. I don't want to become a dark one. I don't want to become nothing."

We all look at him, ashamed. It is the most heartbreaking, honest thing I've heard since we've been here. I don't want to lose myself either. I don't want my soul to disperse into oblivion. I don't want to become a dark one—an aggressive, soulless creature that feeds off other life forces to survive. Looking at where I am now, it's hard to believe I had the life that I've had.

I look toward Daphne, who has been stone silent since we've been here. She has her arms crossed and her head facing downward. She suddenly looks up, making immediate eye contact with me.

I ask her, "What do you want to do, Daphne? Do you want to keep moving forward?"

She breaks eye contact, reverting her eyes to the ground. Phoenix walks over to her and places his hands on her shoulders. She lowers her head, but Phoenix lifts her face up, forcing her eyes to meet his own.

He speaks in a stern but calming tone. "Daphne, I know you're scared. We are all scared, but now we're up against our personal demons. If we stay scared and hidden, we're going to lose. Our souls are at stake here, and we have to be stronger than we were when we were alive. This is our last chance to make things right. What's it going to be: trying or dying?"

Daphne stares into his eyes with mascara tears streaming down the side of her face. She nods her head and speaks. "Yes. I'm in. I'll try, you guys."

It's weird hearing her voice for the first time. It's slightly high-pitched, but hits the eardrum softly. Phoenix smiles and gives her a pat on the back before letting her go. I can't believe she just spoke like that because he told her to. If his charm is this good in the afterlife, I can only imagine his real story.

Craig breaks the moment by saying, "So how does this work? Are we supposed to talk about our feelings and hope for the magic crystal ball to come back?"

I almost call him an asshole, but I don't because I can tell he's speaking out of fear. Instead, I say, "Actually that's exactly what we should do. We should all just—" Before I can finish, the ball of light flies right past us, traveling out of the bedroom. The doorway suddenly lights up, radiating the room with a bright side to this dark picture.

I look at all their stunned faces and say, "Come on, guys. Before we lose it."

We all run through the bedroom door and come to a complete halt when we notice where we are.

* * *

We find ourselves in an empty hospital room. It's daylight, with sun rays forcing their way through the blinds, casting light throughout the room. There is an empty bed with an IV, monitors, and medical instruments all around it. We all go our own way to observe in awe, and I attempt to make sense of this. I try to touch the bed, but the barrier prevents me.

Craig looks to me and asks, "Why are we here?"

"I don't know," I say because I am just as clueless as he is at this point. "Do you remember this place?" I ask.

"Nope. I haven't been here before," he replies.

Suddenly, a pregnant woman appears on the bed. She's lying on her back, legs spread wide open, ready to give birth.

"Mama?" Craig utters in shock.

A man appears next to the pregnant woman, holding her hand.

"Oh shit, that's my dad!" cries Craig.

Craig runs over to the bed and tries to touch his father, but he's blocked by the barrier. He watches his father looking into his mother's eyes, comforting her, guiding her to give birth to him. He stands there gazing at his parents, awestruck by the sight.

A doctor and two nurses appear next to the bed, unveiling the whole scene. We are witnessing Craig's birth. I turn to Craig, who is just as captured as the rest of us. You could hear a pin drop, but even if we heard it, that would not be enough for us to turn away from this. It feels so weird. I am experiencing a memory with him. A very beautiful memory—a complete contrast to the previous memory. The death, then the birth, then everything in between. I really don't know what to expect at this point. I just hope I'm ready for what comes next. I hope we all get through this.

Craig's mother gives that final, life-changing push, and out comes Craig. The doctor cuts the cord and holds him, examining him as the newborn is kicking and screaming. He was a small baby boy, with tiny curls already growing on his almond-shaped head. He's a very loud screamer, his voice beaming in the air, crashing into the ears like a shooting bullet. "Congratulations. You guys have a beautiful, healthy baby boy."

The doctor gives baby Craig to the nurses to have him cleaned. His mother looks exhausted but relieved and very happy.

"Y'all hurry up with my son. I wanna hold him with my wife," his father demands.

A few moments later, the nurse brings Craig back wrapped in a blanket. His mother takes him into her arms, and it was as if all her troubles went away. Tears run down her right cheek as she admires him. "Hi, sweet pea. I'm your mama. This is your daddy, and we love you. Welcome to the world, baby."

She kisses him on the cheek and hugs him with all the love she could give.

"Hey, quit hogging my son, woman," his dad jests.

His mother laughs lightheartedly. She places Craig in his father's arms. He begins to rock him back and forth while humming.

"Wow. My parents looked so happy to have me. Like they loved me. I wish it had stayed that way," Craig says.

"So, you're saying it's all your parents' fault?" Phoenix questions.

"Oh, I see. White people can bitch about their parents their whole lives, and it's normal. A black guy does it, and he's a complainer."

"Yeah, that's exactly what I meant. You have no right at all to complain about your oppression," Phoenix says with a sarcastic undertone.

"Okay, now you're just being an asshole," Craig snaps.

I think they are both being assholes and ruining a particularly nice moment in Craig's eventually fucked up life. I don't know how many happy memories he has. At least his life starts off positive. I only see a glass half-full here.

Phoenix speaks. "Okay, first of all, we are literally walking the footsteps of your life. If I'm supposed to be here witnessing this with you, I assume you need my perspective along with everyone else's. I just think blaming your parents is a cop-out. We are all responsible for our outcomes. We have to own it."

"Let me guess; all this wisdom came from your parents?" Craig asks, crossing his arms.

"My mom died when I was fourteen in a fucked-up way, and my dad was hardly around to console," Phoenix reveals.

Releasing his arms and throwing his hands in the air, Craig replies, "And that didn't affect you at all?"

"Yeah it did, asshole, but my parents aren't the reason I am here. I made a choice, and you made the same one. Now we get to experience all over again what choices we got wrong. Blaming other people is the first mistake you make. I speak from experience," Phoenix says.

"This is worse than the time I spent in county jail," Craig says, letting out a frustrated sigh.

"Tell me about it," Phoenix says, chuckling.

I'm the first to react to his comment. "Ha! No way. How does a firefighter find himself behind bars?" I ask, attempting to lighten the mood.

"A lot of alcohol, and I let this guy get to me. Just another stupid bar fight," Phoenix reminisces.

"Did you win?" I ask, egging the story on.

"Oh yeah. I might have had a night in jail, but he spent the night in the hospital." Phoenix chuckles. "Winning a bar fight isn't worth going to jail. Sometimes it's best to walk away."

Craig speaks. "It's always a lose-lose situation. You stand up for yourself and fight, then you get thrown in jail. You don't, then you get ridiculed. People call you a coward. It's a lose-lose. A double-edged sword."

"Hey, guys," Daphne says. We all turn around to find the ball of light flying around the room. It flies out of the room and into the hallway, lighting up the doorway before disappearing.

"Come on, guys!" I shout as I run away. I run past the door and stop dead in my tracks when I see where I am. I'm not in the hospital anymore. I'm in a house. I'm in a living room, specifically. The others arrive, and they are caught off guard as well—Craig the most. He walks around the room, observing every inch like a forensic scientist.

"It's exactly how I remember it. It's like I'm on the set of the movie of my own life. This is my home—where it all started for me. Why do I have to be first? I feel like the black guy who always dies first in horror movies."

"But you're dead," I say, obviously.

"Exactly," Craig says. "Black guy always dies, and you're a black woman, so there's very little hope for you too."

I don't laugh at this stereotype, knowing how true it is on so many levels. Black people are always treated like we're expendable in movies and reality, unfortunately. I guess that's why they say art is just a reflection of life.

"Have you already forgotten about Max?" Phoenix asks, reminding us of his non-presence.

We all look at him with our own personal affliction. I can still see him being dragged away by the dark ones, how they swarmed him, how scared he must have been, and how we left him behind.

4

Suddenly, a boy appears on the floor. He can't be more than five years old. A toddler appears next to him with Legos surrounding him. The boys begin playing, the oldest building a rocket ship. The younger brother puts one of the pieces in his mouth.

"Dru, get that out of ya mouth! You gonna mess up my piece!" The older brother yanks the piece out of the toddler's hand.

"That's me and my little brother. I had to watch out for him. Anything my siblings did wrong, I had to be punished for it. It's the curse of being an older sibling," Craig says.

Craig's mom stomps into the living room with his father closely on her tail. "Baby, let's talk about this. We can work this out," his father says, desperately.

"No! We can't! You made sure of that when you got that tramp pregnant. I take care of you and this family every day. Y'all are my life, and you dishonored me and your kids. I wish I had never married you, and I hope that bitch gets herpes from the next dick she sucks and spreads it to you first!" His mother walks out of the house, slamming the door behind her, and the boys start crying.

We all look to Craig, and he seems a little disturbed, as he should be. The whole experience is hard to witness. He puts his head down, hiding his shame.

"My mother was never the same after that day. All she did was drink, work, and garden after that. She wanted to forgive him, but seeing my half-sister was a constant reminder of my dad's affair and how she wasn't enough," Craig reveals somberly.

"None of this is your fault," Phoenix says in sincerity.

"Knowing that doesn't take the memories away," he replies.

Everyone suddenly disappears from the living room. Craig's parents appear on the couch, smoking and drinking beer. Craig appears in the center of the room. He's a little older—maybe about ten years old, but definitely an adolescent. A young girl suddenly appears sitting next to him. She couldn't be older than five years old; this must be his half-sister. Oh boy.

The little girl gets up and walks over to her father. "Daddy, can you help me with my homework? I don't get it."

"I can't, baby. I just got off work, and I gotta get ready for my next job in an hour," the father explains, indifferently.

Craig's mother speaks. "Craig, help your HALF-SISTER with her homework."

Craig's father laughs at her contempt, shaking his head and taking a swig of his beer.

"But mama, I haven't got my work done yet," young Craig pleads.

"Boy, you do as I say before I get up and slap you so hard, you lose the taste out of your disobedient tongue!" his mother snaps. He quickly grabs his little sister, and they run out of the room.

The ball of light appears flying in a circle right above where the kids were sitting. The light flies through the front door, disappearing right in front of us. The doorway shines a big, white, flashing light, causing instant captivation. I feel hypnotized as I walk through the door and into the unknown.

* * *

The light dies down, and we notice that we are in a classroom. It has at least two-dozen chairs, with music stands facing the teacher's desk.

"This is my band class. I was in high school, I think; it was so long ago. I always liked band. It seemed like it didn't like me back, though." Craig says.

A full classroom of students appears with instruments and music sheets in front of them. They're all socializing among themselves, with a few being loud and obnoxious. The teacher walks into the classroom, going straight to her desk. I notice teenage Craig in the back of the room practicing his tuba. He looks different here. For one, he so skinny here that his tuba looks like it's going to crush him, but he seems to have complete control over it.

I say, "You were pretty good. Did you continue to play?"

"No. I wasn't good enough for a scholarship. They made the tryouts impossible that year. Only two people got it, and four got partial scholarships," Craig replies.

The teacher speaks. "Attention, class! Attention! I know I have already assigned section leaders for summer band camp. It has come to my knowledge that one of our students that I had picked to lead the tuba section is transferring schools. Anyways, I went back through everyone's audition, and I discovered that Craig Simpson had the highest score. So Craig, if you would like to become section leader, it is yours."

"Yeah, I'll do it. This way everyone can learn from me, and finally get better," teenage Craig says, confidently. He looks over at a pretty girl with amber colored skin sitting next to him. "Dee Dee, you have any questions, you come to me, girl. I'll be there."

"Okay, stalker. Let the girl breathe. Damn!" a white guy sitting behind him says. A few students around the classroom laugh at his remark.

"Whatever. You're just hating cause I'm as fine as wine. Plus, me and Dee Dee belong together. We're the only black people we know that love astronomy," Craig replies.

"Boy, stop playing with me. You know you're like my brother from another Baptist mother," says Dee Dee.

"Okay, students; playtime is over. Time to get to work. Homecoming isn't going to play itself! How bout we warm up with 'Seven Nation Army' by The White Stripes?"

They all scream out their excitement in unison, and the teacher begins a countdown: "A five, six, seven, go!"

The tuba section begins playing that famous riff, the trumpet section soon follows and begins harmonizing. The bass snare finds its position in the song, building the anticipation for the rest of the band. The music soon clashes together, and you can feel the teenage angst bleeding between the notes dancing around the room. The sound is loud, clear, and epic. You can hear every variation of each note; it's like being inside a speaker.

This is the first song I've heard since being here. It almost makes me feel alive again. I start bopping my head with the music. I look over at our Craig, and he's already a step ahead of me, dancing around, acting like he's playing his tuba. This is the first time I've seen him come out of his shell. Suddenly, I realize that my judgment of him seemed a little premature. He can be an asshole, but even assholes own a soul.

Phoenix starts snapping his fingers to the beat. Even Daphne begins swaying her hips around, smiling at the beat. The song concludes, and everything and everyone disappears from the room, leaving a deafening silence so profound that they should consider adding a negative level to the volume button. The power of music.

Craig speaks. "That was some serious nostalgia right there. We had the time of our lives in band class. Only time in my life when I felt good about myself and where I was. At first, I only joined because of that girl. She went to my church, and she was the prettiest girl I had ever seen. If only I knew. When I had joined, though, I ended up loving it, and it kept me out of trouble, unlike my siblings."

"Your band seemed really disciplined," I say.

"Yeah, we tried. Were you into music?" Craig asks me.

I laugh a little at his question. "Oh, yeah. I lived and breathed music. I was the lead singer in a rock band before I died."

"Nice. I'm impressed," Craig replies. He waves his hand in the air to give me a high-five, and then we all notice his hands. Spots of light are flashing through his skin and slowly spreading down his arms.

"Ahh! What the hell is this?" Craig cries.

"How do you feel? Does it hurt?" Phoenix asks as he runs over, yanking his arm.

"Hey! Careful, before you rip my arms off," Craig says in a stern, frustrated tone.

"Sorry. I forget my own strength sometimes. I've only ever said that to women up until this point."

"Shut up!" Craig says. I laugh at the subtle insult. He does seem to overreact to everything that happens to him, from what I've seen. But this is a serious issue. Or is it?

"Well, it obviously doesn't hurt too much. This happened just now after our jam session. Music is such a positive art form. For a moment, you had somehow found yourself through music, and I don't know...earned some spiritual points," I say. "I don't feel anything negative, do you?"

"No," Craig answers.

"The spirit world is testing us. We have to relive crucial moments in our lives, and if we pass, we get to move on. If we fail, then we become a dark one and go away forever. It makes sense. The more you go through your memories, Craig, the closer you get to moving on. So, if you can hold onto those feelings, maybe your whole body will turn into light, and can move onto something better. You're lucky to be picked first," I conclude, crossing my arms confidently.

"Lucky? I have to share my life with people I didn't even know during my lifetime. All while you guys are judging me, and my life is only going to get worse from here."

"What are you complaining about? I still have on my nightgown. I'm just glad I didn't die naked," I say to myself.

Phoenix overhears me. "What are you complaining about? I'm still dressed in my uniform. What fire am I going to put out in this place?" he asks, whispering to keep the conversation between us.

"Well, you can always provide your service as a stripper for all the depressed, lonely, dead women in this place," I say, jokingly.

This makes Phoenix laugh out loud. "Believe it or not, you're not the first to present that idea. Men get objectified too," he says, nudging my arm playfully with his elbow.

I chuckle to myself before turning my attention back to Craig. "Craig, listen; your life so far has had its hardships. You have nothing to be embarrassed about. You're not the most fucked up person in this place. We have a woman who won't speak unless she has too," I say, looking over at Daphne, who is standing away from the group. "I probably come across crazy myself for killing myself in these rags. Look at Phoenix." Phoenix laughs when he hears his name. "We are all awkward freaks. Believe me when I say that considering what I gave up, I feel like a fucking idiot for throwing it all away," I say.

The light shows itself once more, flying circles around Craig. It flies out of the room, illuminating the doorway. We walk through the door with little hesitation. I think we are finally getting used to the routine.

* * *

We find ourselves in the woods. Slender but tall pine trees surround us. Rays of sunlight peek through the leaves that are flowing graciously against the wind. I wish I could feel the wind or the sun. I wish I could smell the aroma of pine and dirt. It's the first time we've been "outside." I can't help but miss the feeling of nature. I'll never get to go back there. None of us will.

Craig speaks. "This is where we had band camp. I wonder if they are going to show me getting laid here. That's a memory I wouldn't mind reliving."

"Let's hope not," Phoenix and I say simultaneously. I smile to myself at this, but say nothing to acknowledge it, though I can feel Phoenix's eyes on me as if he's waiting for me to respond.

Teenage Craig appears by a tree in front of us. Dee Dee appears, standing in front of him.

"Oh, no. Not this one," our Craig pleads.

Teenage Craig grabs Dee Dee's hand. He looks her in the eyes and goes for the kiss. She turns her head away, yanking her hand from his in the process.

"No. Stop, Craig. I told you, you're like my brother. I'll never like you in that way. I'm not trying to hurt your feelings, but this has to stop," Dee Dee pleads.

"What about all the things we have in common? I'm always there for you when you need a friend, so why am I not good enough for you now?" teenage Craig says harshly as he takes in all that rejection.

"It's not that you aren't good enough," she answers.

"Then how come you always push me out?" he interjects.

"I haven't pushed you out, Craig, because you're not in. You'll never be. I'm sorry. I gotta go." Dee Dee runs off back to the cabins, leaving Craig to himself. You can read the devastation on his face. He walks away from the camp, I'm assuming to reflect.

"Harsh," Phoenix blurts out.

"Yeah, harsh," Craig says. "She never even gave me a chance. I did everything for her: helped her out with homework, gave her all my notes in class. I only joined band in the first place for her. But she wanted the stupid jocks and the stupid bad boys. I treated her way better than any of her boyfriends ever did, but because I didn't get into trouble, I wasn't cool enough. Fuck her."

"Okay, she was your first love, and she turned you down. It happens. We are all stupid at that age, and she wasn't attracted to you. It's not her fault. She can't help that," I say in her defense.

"She's stupid. She didn't end up doing anything with her life, anyway," Craig says in a bitter tone.

"Ouch!" Craig suddenly yells. He looks at his glowing extremities. The being of light flies past us and into one of the cabins. I take the lead in running after it.

I reach the cabin, and the door frame is illuminated as before. The others soon follow, and we all cross together.

* * *

We find ourselves in a school stadium with banners everywhere reading, "Class of 2006."

A room full of people standing around appears. Families are congratulating the graduates, teachers are wishing the parents well, camera lights are flashing around the room, and a whole lot of other nonsense that you expect at a graduation.

An eighteen-year-old Craig appears in front of us. He's wearing a crimson red gown and holding a matching cap in his hand. His friend, Brendon, appears next to him along with two other boys who are all wearing the same graduate gowns.

"We did it! We're free!" one of the boys yell as he throws his hat into the air.

"Guys, this is it; we won't be seeing each other much after this. What are we going to do with ourselves?" Brendon asks.

"I'm going to art school for graphic design," Craig says proudly.

"I am too, but I'm staying here in state. I'm lucky I got a scholarship at all," Brendon says.

"Well, I'm going to a better school, so I can be the best. It's out of state, but I'll visit for Christmas. Besides, I'm going to be too busy chasing girls and earning my degree. I can't wait to get out of here!" young Craig screams boastfully.

"To 2006!" one of the boys yell. They all begin yelling and pushing each other, expressing their happiness of achievement.

"Wow. How hopeful I looked then. I had no idea the shit storm life would throw at me," Craig says.

"No one does, Craig. No one," I say.

Suddenly, everyone in the room disappears except for the former "Craig." The whole room illuminates with a blinding light, rendering the invisible barrier useless. Out of reflex, we all cover our eyes. The light dims, we look up, and young adult Craig is staring intensely at us. He's wearing jeans and a wrinkled white T-shirt.

He starts running into what looks like another doorway. He runs through, causing it to illuminate that warm, foreign light that invites us to join. The light gives a false sense of consolation, though. There is no such thing as a happy memory in a place like this. When you kill yourself, your memories are only bitter or bittersweet.

5

We walk through, stepping into a college classroom. Students appear, walking out of the classroom and conversing among themselves. A professor appears, wiping the dry erase board, discarding his lesson plan. We see a frantic Craig running toward the teacher.

"Class is over. All work was to be turned in before class ends. That's been a rule all semester," the teacher says as he's still cleaning his board.

College Craig speaks. "I know. I'm so sorry. I've just been so stressed trying to keep up with other classes, and I haven't eaten a proper meal in days and—"

"No exceptions," the teacher interjects.

"But you said this assignment is worth a third of our grade. If I can't turn this in, I won't pass your class, and I can't afford to fail any more classes. Please. I'm here, and I have my assignment ready to turn in. I don't care what points you take off, just please," Craig pleads.

The teacher turns around and takes Craig's art assignment. He looks at the drawing and hands it back to him. "Failing this class might not be the worst thing that ever happened to you. Your assignment is a C at best, and if I take it now, I would have to deduct late points, and you would end up with a failing grade anyway. I'm not saying this to be mean; I'm just telling you the truth. You are not a good artist. You are average at best. Save yourself time and money, and try something else," the professor says with indifference.

"No. That's bullshit. Your job is to teach me! You're supposed to help me! What the hell am I paying you for?" younger Craig yells argumentatively.

"Yes, my job is to teach. I can't make you show up to class ON TIME. That is up to you. LEARNING is on you. Learn to take some responsibility." The teacher quickly packs his things and begins to walk away.

"Fine, then! I don't need to be talked down to by some professor. You ain't shit. You ain't more successful than anybody else I know. I can do better."

"Good. Go be better," the teacher says, unfazed, as he's walking out of the classroom.

The former Craig slams his stuff on the floor before stomping out. I turn to our Craig, who looks a bit disappointed. It's a hard blow.

"I left college that day. I couldn't keep my grades up, and I couldn't apply for more student loans, so I left. I don't regret leaving, though. I hated that school. I spent all that time and work to get nothing. It was a big waste of my time," he says.

"Well, it seems like you didn't put the work in, to be honest," Phoenix says.

"You don't know. You weren't in my shoes," Craig replies.

"You showed up at the last minute on the day your assignment was due and expected him to give you a pass. It was worth a third of your grade. I would think that if you worked as hard as you said, you would have made it to class on time that day," says Phoenix.

"Man, whatever. You don't know anything," Craig says dismissively.

"Okay, then why were you late?" Phoenix asks, crossing his arms.

"I overslept! Don't tell me you never overslept before. Oh, that's right; when you have white privilege, you always get a pass," Craig says.

"Yeah, I'm so privileged being in here in the same position as you. I've seen more white males in this hellhole than anyone. We must have really squandered our white privilege if our lives were so easy and we had everything handed to us," Phoenix replies.

"Hell yeah, yo dumbasses squandered it. You had the most to benefit from life, and yet you chose to end it. That tells me y'all are lost causes that ride on the coattails of your grandfathers," Craig says, trying to get under Phoenix's skin.

"Oh yeah? Well unlike your grandfather, you were too weak to live out your life. Don't call out the kettle for being black," Phoenix says.

Exasperated at them both, I say, "Okay, you both need to stop! Watching you both quarrel over whose struggle was the worst is fucking insufferable and stupid. We got bigger issues than this and arguing isn't going to get us anywhere. You two need to find some common ground or just not speak at all."

"You know what, you're right. Let's move on. I wasn't right for art school. There, I said it. This ain't even my whole life," Craig says.

The ball of light flies in front of us, gracing us with its presence once again. It flies out of the room, and we follow.

* * *

We find ourselves in an apartment. We see the former Craig in his early twenties, sitting at a table with a group of friends, laughing and having a good time.

They are playing a card game and drinking liquor. There is a catchy rap song playing in the background, the kind of music you hear at any house party.

"I always knew you would be back," Craig's friend, Brendon, says.

"Yeah, yeah, yeah. You're just glad y'all have a place to go outside of your parents' house now," younger Craig replies.

"No, we're just glad we can bust your balls about going to art school. Tell me: how many pastel drawings got you laid?" one of his friends jokes.

"It wasn't what you think it was. I'm just glad to be home, and that I landed my job. I got all I need right here," younger Craig says with confidence.

"Except a girlfriend. We all know you didn't get laid up there," Brendon says, and they share a laugh.

"Man, I miss that apartment. I miss that time. The only time in my life when things were going right. This was the best I had it," our Craig admits. A tear falls onto his left cheek. He touches the invisible barrier, longing to be there. I know for a fact that he's wishing he could redo it all over again. He wishes he could go back. But we can never go back.

We see the past Craig get up, muttering something about a bathroom break, before heading toward it. He opens the bathroom door, and it is suddenly drowned with light. I guess life really is just one door after another. We all walk through, closing a layer of his past behind us.

6

We arrive at an empty restaurant. It must be at least a four-star restaurant based off the design alone. There's a beautiful glass water fountain with stone trim placed in the center of the restaurant. Black tablecloths top the tables with formally placed silverware and dinnerware. The plates are perfectly centered with diamond folded napkins on top. The lights are dim, slightly blending with the marble ceiling and gold wallpaper.

People suddenly appear, casually having dinner and enjoying themselves. Classical music can be heard in the background, filling the room with soft melodies.

We see a twenty-something version of Craig sitting with a woman. By their formal attire, I can assume they're on a date. This place is too fancy for a first date, so this is a special occasion.

"Oh, great! Not this heffer!" Craig shouts in anger. "She broke my heart, and I was so good to her. Would have always been there for her, but no, I wasn't good enough. Story of my life. I can't even watch this. I'd rather watch myself die again."

"Was the breakup that bad?" I ask.

"See for yourself," he mutters, turning his back on himself. We turn our attention back to them.

"Craig, you shouldn't have brought me here; this place is too nice. You shouldn't have done all of this," the young woman says.

"Baby, don't be silly. You are my woman, and I like spoiling you. In fact, I love making you happy; it makes me happy," past Craig says. He gets up from his seat and drops down to one knee.

"Um...Craig, what are you doing?"

He reveals a heart-shaped, wooden engagement ring box.

"Craig, wait! I can't let you do this," she says.

Confusion draws on his face as he finds his seat. "What's going on? I had this all planned out. We've been together for three years now, and I thought this was the next step for us. Talk to me, Jerrika." His voice cracks.

"It's not you or anything you did. I haven't been honest with you, and I was wrong. I've been seeing someone else for the past year. I do have love for you. You took care of me, and I will always cherish our time together," she says.

"So, you love him more, is that what you're telling me?" he spits.

Jerrika takes a deep breath as if she's preparing her next words carefully. "Craig, I'm pregnant with his child. He already knows, and we're going to be a family. I know this is a lot, and I'm so sorry."

The past Craig sits there heartbroken. Tears begin to fill his eyes. He gets up from the table and storms away. Jerrika calls after him, but it falls on deaf ears, and he is soon out of the building.

"What a bitch!" I say in disgust. That was the most brutal breakup I have ever witnessed up until this point. No one deserves to be treated like that. That's just fucked up.

"I know, but she was just the beginning. One way or another, each girl I've dated has taken advantage of me. It's like I had the word SUCKER stamped on my forehead and only whores could see it," Craig says bitterly.

"I have to give you props for walking away like you did. Not every man would have done that," says Phoenix in a way that makes me think he might have experienced something similar.

The ball of light flies past us, leading us to the exit of the restaurant.

* * *

Following the light leads us to an empty hotel hallway. I can see an elevator at the end. The elevator door opens, and we see the former "Craig" walk out carrying stuffed animals and shopping bags in his hands.

"Just... Why me?" our Craig asks rhetorically.

A young woman is with him, holding her purse and a room key. They walk down the hallway, laughing and joking around. They stop at room 706 and let themselves in. The doorway lights up again, cuing us to walk through it.

We oblige, quickly walking through to see the other side. I expected to find Craig and his girlfriend, but the room is empty. The hotel room is very standard: two queen-sized beds, a boxed television set, and a mini fridge. The things he was carrying before are laid out on one of the beds. The couple appears on the bed unexpectedly. We all direct our attention to them.

We watch Craig hand the woman a glass of wine. He turns on the television and finds an r&b and soul channel. He turns his attention back to her and takes a sip of his wine.

"Are you having a good time, sweet birthday girl?" he asks her, happily.

"Yes. Today was great. No one ever took me out shopping and to a festival. I'm so glad I met you. It's the best birthday ever," she says before taking a sip of her wine. "So good," she compliments.

"I'm glad I met you too. In fact, I can show you better than I can tell you, Tonya." He sets his drink down and starts kissing her neck, and his hands begin roaming around her body. I didn't know the spirit world would show our intimate lives as well. Oh, no; I don't think I can deal with that. That would break me apart. I couldn't. I'm having a hard time watching this, and it's not even my experience.

Craig kisses her lips, and she hesitates at first, but soon jumps on board. They begin making out and caressing each other.

I look over at our Craig, and he's just looking at the floor. His reaction is surprising. I always thought men loved reliving their sexual experiences. He doesn't look happy at all. Does an audience really bother him that much? I guess I'll find out soon enough. Let's hope.

"You wanna suck it?" the past Craig asks briefly between kisses.

"Yeah, I'll do it," she says.

Oh, this is so going down. This is like a live porn show. Like I went to go see a play, and they had sex in front of an audience. This is too weird, and I feel wrong for watching, but like a bad car accident, I can't bring myself to look away. I must know how it ends.

He takes off his shirt, and she does the same. He seems to be in average shape; not as slim as he was in college, but not overweight. She's a very pretty girl with mocha toned skin and petite frame. She sits down on the bed and pulls his pants down, revealing his Batman boxers. She giggles and pulls his boxers down, revealing his member. Her eyes open wide, and her facial expression changes to disgust.

"Oh my God, you're uncircumcised! You never told me that. That's disgusting! You've been sweating, and oh my God!" she yells. She jumps up and throws her clothes back on.

"What just... What just happened? Hey, wait, wait, wait. I didn't think it mattered. It looks the same when I'm hard. I'm clean. I took a shower this morning. I can take another one. I don't care, just wait."

"No. You should have told me. I know how it looks hard; you sent me pictures, remember," she says, walking away from him.

He speeds in front of her. "Wait, don't go. Let's talk about this. We had such a great day today, and I've been waiting to be with you for almost a year!" he weeps.

"I'm not leaving; you are! This is my room. I can't do this tonight. I need to think about all of this," she replies.

"I did not spend ten months getting to know you, spend my hard-earned money to pay your bills, drive over a thousand miles to see you on your birthday, and take you out to do all kinds of fun shit for this night to end like this! I earned your heart. What more do I have to do for you to see that I love you and want to be with you?" he yells at her, letting out all of his frustration and anger.

She retorts, "You may have done all of that, but that don't mean you have direct access to this. This is my body, and if I don't want to have sex with you, that's something you got to accept. You can be mad all you want, but you were the one who spent ten months doing all of that. No one made you do any of this. No one made you keep your 'condition' a secret from me. I think you should leave and take some responsibility for yourself." She opens the door and crosses her arms, awaiting for him to leave.

"So, that's it? You're just gonna kick me out after I did... Bitch, you are fucking crazy! I swear, I'll never date online again. The stupid people you meet! You silly ass bitch!"

He grabs all the things he bought and leaves. She runs out of the room yelling, "You still have your smegma-ridden dick exposed! Who you calling stupid, bitch?"

This is actually the first time I have ever seen an uncircumcised penis. I always thought that was an uncommon thing, but to each their own. But wow, that did not turn out the way I expected.

"Wow," Phoenix says, putting his hand over his mouth awkwardly.

"How come you're not circumcised?" I ask with genuine curiosity.

"My parents didn't see the point. I agree with them. There's no difference, medically speaking; it's just for show. People think it looks better, but did you know that most women claim the sex is way better with an uncircumcised penis?"

"Women don't say that," Daphne says.

We all look at her because, well, she spoke. I wonder if she speaks from experience. Maybe I'll get to see her story before it's my turn.

"Why didn't you tell her that? Ten months of not seeing each other, I would think you guys would've had a lot of naughty phone conversations at least," I ask, curiously.

"I didn't think it would matter, honestly. Now I know that you women just want what you see in magazines," Craig replies, agitated.

"Not all women are superficial. She's seriously overreacted though," I say, shaking my head at his unfortunate circumstances.

The doorway lights up again. "Thank you!" Craig yells, running out of the hotel room.

We all give each other a look before following him to the next stage of his miserable life. Here it goes again.

7

We find ourselves in a lunch break room. There are a few tables and chairs, a refrigerator, and a limestone countertop with a microwave, coffeemaker, and condiments on it. The walls are a pearl gray shade. The color reminds me of prison cell walls; not the kind of work environment where creativity is involved.

"This was the last decent job I ever had: machine operating. It was hard work, but I got paid well and promoted fairly quickly," Craig says with a slight sadness.

"What happened? Did they let you go?" I ask.

"No. It's complicated," Craig replies.

Past Craig walks into the break room along with two other guys. Here, he resembles the Craig we know. He's wearing blue coveralls and brown steel-toed boots. His face is fuller, his belly is larger, and his beard has grown in. I guess he stopped caring after the last girl, but who can blame him. That breakup sucked, but sometimes you must learn things the hard way. For him, it seems like he always learned the hard way.

The men all sit and begin eating their lunches together. Craig gets up and walks over to the refrigerator to retrieve his drink. One of the other guys walks over to him.

"Hey, Craig, can I talk to you for a second?" the guy asks.

"Yeah, what's up, man?" he replies.

"I just wanted to let you know, since you my boy, that I was in a meeting last week with the boss. I overheard them talking about laying people off, and I know you were one of the last hired," the guy says.

"No. They just promoted me; they ain't gonna fire me. Why give me a bonus? I do good work and get everything done on time. I feel safe."

"I heard them say yo name, man. They said a bunch of names. Hell, even the ones they keeping are getting demoted to part time. I don't know about you, but I'm looking for another job. Come next week, a lot of people are getting laid off, and yo black ass—as good of a worker as you are—is still replaceable," the guy says and walks away. The former Craig grabs his things and walks out of the break room.

"So you were laid off?" I ask, trying to put the pieces together.

"No, I quit. I thought that since they were laying people off, it would look better if I put in my notice than to be laid off."

"But you would have been eligible for unemployment if you let them lay you off," I say.

"I figured I should quit while I still had a good recommendation. You're a woman; it's easy for you to find work. It was hard enough for me to stay out of jail, let alone keep a job," Craig replies.

"What ended up happening after you quit? Did people get laid off like he said?" I ask.

"Yes. Wait, no. People got fired for attendance reasons, but it turns out no one got laid off," Craig admits.

"So you got played," I say, shaking my head.

"No, no, no. I may have reacted impulsively, but I was not played," Craig says in defense.

"Did your friend get fired?" Phoenix asks.

"No. As far as I know, he stayed there until the day I died," Craig says, as if a revelation has come upon him.

"Yeah, you were played. I'm sorry. It sucks man. Nobody likes to be taken advantage of, but it happened to you here. You just have to accept that sometimes," Phoenix says.

Craig doesn't say anything. He turns his back to us and puts his head down. Phoenix walks over to him and puts his hand on his shoulder.

"You don't have to feel bad. We've all made mistakes." Phoenix says.

"The damn job should have told me to stay. If I were as valuable as they claimed, they would have asked me to stay," Craig says.

I roll my eyes at him. How hard is it for him to admit when he's wrong? Now is not the time. In fact, this is our last chance, and he can't take any responsibility. I know I'm weak, but I'm strong enough to admit when I'm wrong.

"That's not an employer's obligation. Unfortunately, we're all replaceable in a professional setting. You chose to leave. Stop blaming everyone else for your problems because in the end, you put yourself here. None of us are in the right here," I speak.

"My entire life was wrong! I tried to live an honest life, and look where it fucking got me!" Craig yells, clenching his fists together with a vibrant, white light beaming through the cracks of his skin.

I speak sincerely. "Life is a big test, and we failed. Now we get to go back and see what we got wrong. If we don't learn from our mistakes and fail again, we won't have any more chances. We don't get another retake.

Forgive yourself, Craig; that's all you have to do. You're not a bad person at all. We all saw that you were capable of great things."

"This is my life; you don't get to preach to me about how I react to it. You're just a know-it-all, but you're here too, just like me, so keep your mouth shut!" he replies.

I stomp over to him and stare in his coffee brown eyes. "Excuse me for giving a shit about your existence. You can push us all away if you want but remember it's your soul on the line right now. No one can save you, if you don't want to save yourself."

"Yeah, it's easy to act sanctimonious when you're on the other side of the story. Don't forget: your story is coming up too, honey."

"Craig, your hands!" Phoenix yells.

I take notice of his hands as well. They are not glowing anymore. Instead, they're gray. Gray patches spread down his hands and onto his arms. Just like the dark ones. He's already on his way. Oh shit! I didn't think it would happen this quickly. It can't be too late, can it?

"Oh, no! This ain't happening! This ain't happening! Why do my arms feel twice as heavy? What does this mean? I can't go through this!" Craig whines.

The ball of light appears, flying in circles around Craig. He reaches out to grab it, but is only met with air.

"You can't do this to me! I was wronged! I'm the victim! The world was against me!" Craig fusses.

The ball of light flies out of the break room, illumining the doorway. Craig sprints after it. I have never seen him run that fast, not even when the dark ones were chasing us. I give Phoenix a worried look, and he appears just as concerned as I am about all of this. Daphne looks at us briefly before exiting.

Phoenix grabs my hand. "Come on. We have to keep going."

I nod in concurrence. We walk through the doorway, still hand in hand. I squeeze his hand a little harder as we cross through to combat the shakiness my extremities are experiencing due to my fear of what's to come.

* * *

We find ourselves in a living room. There is a nice faux stone fireplace with empty picture frames on top. The lights are off, while the fire is burning and crackling. I wish I could smell the firewood burning, but I can't. We're on the other side.

I look over at Craig, and he's just standing there staring at the fire. Pictures of a man and woman start to appear in the picture frames. Pictures of weddings and vacations and life achievements. I recognize the faces from Craig's past, but I can't tell who they are. I don't see Craig in any picture though, so this must not be his house.

The man and woman in the picture walk into the living room and sit on the living room couch. They are both enjoying a cup of hot chocolate with marshmallows. Past Craig walks into the room and sits next to them, placing a plate of cookies on the coffee table. Here he appears to be in his mid-thirties because of his developing crow's feet.

"Guys, thanks again for letting me crash here 'til I get back on my feet. It's nice to know that I still have friends," Craig says, taking a sip of his hot chocolate.

"Of course. We all have been through tough times. That's what best friends do: be there for each other," the guy says.

"Speaking of friends, I can't believe you two are married. I mean Brendon, I remember your ex-girlfriend, Gia, and she was just slutty. I remember they used to call her "Road Head." You never had the best taste in women, but here you are, married to Dee Dee," Craig says.

Brendon chuckles and puts his arm around Dee Dee. "Yes, I was an idiot before I met Dee Dee. We hadn't seen each other since our high school graduation. We ran into each other at our college graduation and decided to meet for lunch to catch up. I was lucky she agreed because there were guys just begging for her attention. I could barely get her phone number without someone yelling her name."

"Oh, it wasn't like that," Dee Dee says, laughing.

"Well, that's how I remember it. You're a hard woman to catch. Guys see a beautiful woman and they lose their minds. Nothing else in the world matters when I see you," Brendon gushes.

"Aww, babe. I love you," Dee Dee says. She kisses him lovingly. I notice past Craig avert his eyes when she does, giving off a jealous vibe. It then hits me that Dee Dee was the same girl that rejected him all those years ago. She looks a little different, but the resemblance is still there. She's just more mature and filled out, but in a good way. Brendon has changed too; he's a lot taller and has developed an impressive, muscular build.

So, Craig's high school crush grows up to be even more beautiful than before, and she marries his best friend. That's an unfortunate outcome. They do look happy, though, and they made a beautiful home for themselves.

"It's funny how things change. So how do you like graphic design, Brendon? Are you happy in the field?" Craig asks.

"I love it. I get to be creative, and it pays well. I also have a lot of independence and flexibility. Dee Dee is an author of children's books, and I get to help her illustrate them. It's fun when we get to work together, and it works. She's making a big name for herself with her latest book," he says.

"There he goes again," Dee Dee says, smiling.

"That's great. What's the name of it?" Craig asks.

"Here, I'll show you," Dee Dee says. She hands him a copy of her book.

"*The Bumble in the Bee*. Hmm. Good job on the artwork, Brendon. What's the story about?" Craig asks.

"Well, it's about a bumble bee named Sue whose dream is to become a scout bee. Scout bees get to search for food for the colony, and they pollinate plants. To be a scout bee, you must be a great flier. Sue is awkward and a very clumsy flier, but she won't give up on her dream. It's a short book. Feel free to read it," Dee Dee says excitedly.

"Yeah, I'll skim through it. I'm not a big reader, but it seems like a good story," Craig says.

"Oh, okay. No pressure," Dee Dee says. "Well, Craig, we are heading to bed. Goodnight. Get some rest.

Don't worry; you will find another job soon and get back on your feet. Soon as you do that, I have some friends that are single and ready to mingle."

"Why can't you introduce me to them now? I need love too," Craig says.

"No, you need to focus on yourself first. Trust me; women don't waste time on a guy who doesn't have his life together. You're a great guy with a lot to offer, and I believe in you. Believe in yourself. Goodnight, Craig," Dee Dee says.

Dee Dee and Brendon head upstairs to their bedroom. Craig gets up from the couch and walks over to the fireplace. He examines all their pictures and stops at their wedding picture. He sighs, pours his hot chocolate into the fireplace, and walks out of the living room.

"I can't believe Brendon married Dee Dee. I wanted her, but she didn't give me the time of day. Brendon just randomly encounters her, and she gives him a chance. They only dated for six months before he proposed. Can you believe that?" our Craig says.

"Sounds like you're a hater," Phoenix says. I smile at his comment because it's so true.

"No, I'm not a hater. Yeah, he ended up with the life I wanted, but that's only because he's white. He grew up broke like me, went to all black schools like me, and he still came out better. Why? Because he's a white boy. White men always have it easier. Hell, they own everything!" Craig argues.

"He had the same disadvantages as you, and he made something of himself, and you didn't. You said it yourself. If he worked hard for it, why can't you give him credit for it? He worked and got his degree. He worked to win the love of that woman. You can't be mad at the player for winning when it's a fair game," Phoenix says.

"The game has never been fair to the black man! I don't know why you keep arguing about something you'll never understand," Craig says, shaking his head in exasperation.

"You're right. A lot of white men are privileged. I was one of them. You're right that I don't understand what it's like to be black. All I see here is that he's your friend who gave you his home. You shouldn't be jealous of your friends, especially when they go out of their way to help you," Phoenix says.

The ball of light flies out from the fireplace, startling the hell out of us. It flies out of the living room, making a sharp right before flying upstairs. We follow it to a bedroom with the door way lit up. We quickly walk through without hesitation.

* * *

We see the former Craig sitting by his computer, typing on his desktop. His bedroom is a wreck. There are dirty clothes on the floor, and dirty dishes and fast food bags scattered everywhere. I would think this room was in a different house if I didn't know any better. We walk closer to see what he's typing. He's messaging someone on Facebook. I look a little closer and read the name "Gia." As in Brendon's ex-girlfriend, Gia. What the hell?

"So, what is Brendon's new wife like?" past Craig reads aloud. He begins typing, reciting each word.

"She's not that great. I went to school with her, and she's always been a bitch. She calls herself an author, but I read one of her books, and it was garbage."

My jaw nearly hits the floor, and I look over at Craig, and his head is facing the ground. I'm guessing he's trying to hide his shame. I look over at Phoenix, and he looks pissed off. Daphne has her hand over her mouth in shock. I'm not sure how I look, but I'm pretty upset at all of this. I can't stand a damn phony.

We hear another beep, indicating another Facebook notification. Craig reads it. He responds, reading as he's typing. "They are so lame and boring. Brendon is only a one-minute man, and she's louder than a banshee. I swear I can't wait to get out of here.

When I get my own place, you can come over, and we can show those losers how it's really done."

"Really?" Phoenix asks rhetorically, using a disgusted tone.

"You're a real piece of shit, Craig," Daphne says.

"Fuck you. You're no saint!" Craig speaks in defense.

"No one's perfect here," I interject. "I bet they discovered just how imperfect you really were."

The ball of light appears, flying out of the bedroom back downstairs into the living room.

* * *

We get there and see Craig and Brendon sitting on the couch, playing video games. This is hard to watch after seeing what we saw. Dee Dee stomps into the living room and turns off the game. She holds a phone in Craig's face.

"You lying, sneaky, fucking snake! You have been telling our business and trying to fuck Brendon's ex-girlfriend. Making fun of our sex lives, calling us losers, calling me a bitch! How dare you! We took you in when even your parents wouldn't take you! I cooked dinner every night, making sure you ate. I cleaned up after you and listened to your bullshit, and you disrespect me in my own house! I should kill you! Get the fuck out, and never come back, you son of a bitch!"

"He... What?" Brendon asks, completely dumbfounded.

"Why were you looking through my phone? You had no right to look through my things," past Craig replies nervously, as his weak defense. Dee Dee punches Craig on the nose, causing him to scream in pain.

"If you don't leave in five seconds, I will call the police. I already threw your shit out; it's on the curb. If I ever see you or that fucking slut around here again, I will make you disappear. No one would miss your selfish, manipulative ass anyway. Get out!" Dee Dee screams with a voice so sharp, it slices through you.

"Did you not hear her? Get the fuck out! I can't believe you could treat us like this after twenty years of friendship! I let you into my home. Our home! Just go! Go now! I can't even stand to look at you!" Brendon yells.

Brendon grabs Craig and yanks him out of his chair. Brendon is a pretty big guy, especially compared to Craig. He pushes him toward the door. Craig looks back at them again.

"Don't make me come to that door!" Brendon says. Craig hurries out of the home, leaving them alone.

Dee Dee bursts into tears. Brendon hugs her and kisses the top of her head.

"I can't feel my arms anymore," our Craig says. I look over, and his arms and hands are completely gray. It's even starting to spread to his neck, forming into the shape of flames. That can't be good.

"Craig, just apologize already. Your pride isn't worth losing your soul for," Phoenix pleads.

"Fine. I was wrong. I was jealous of my friends, and it made me feel better to put them down. I didn't think anyone would ever find out. I was wrong!" Craig yells.

Everyone grows silent. Nothing changes on his arms. In fact, it's still spreading across his body.

"Did you mean it?" Phoenix asks.

"Yes, it's the truth. I swear I was jealous, and I wanted to get back at my friend. It was petty, and he didn't deserve that. Dee Dee was just mad that I talked bad about her book. She shouldn't have gone through my stuff anyway. I don't feel bad about her," Craig admits.

"You're just sour because she rejected you all those years ago, man. She didn't deserve that either. It was her house too, or did that not occur to you? You have to let this go. She is not the reason for your pain.

None of those women are. It's still you that made those choices," Phoenix says.

The front doorway lights up. We all make our way through the door, silent as a grave yard.

8

We find ourselves back in the living room of Craig's childhood home. The walls are painted a different color, I think. You can tell the home has been updated. The former Craig appears, sitting on the couch. His father appears, asleep on the recliner, holding a beer can. His father's hair and beard are graying, and his eye bags are drooping, a few of the many gifts that come with stress and aging. His mother appears next, standing in the center of the room, wearing a robe with rollers in her gray hair.

"So, you been looking for a job?" his mom asks intently.

"For the millionth time, Mama, yes. It's hard out there for black men; you know that. Constantly opposed, always disadvantaged," Craig says.

"Excuses, excuses. Boy, I did not raise no sorry ass son. You're the first born; your siblings are supposed to be looking up to you. Instead, they think you're a joke. What happened, baby? Why did you stop trying? I know we are fucked up, but that's between me and your father. You need to take some responsibility too, son. Here."

She hands him a pamphlet. "What's this?" Craig asks.

"It's from the community college. They have cheap classes you can take that're quick. CNA classes are only three months. They also have tech courses for six months to a year. I think this is the best option for you. You need to learn a new skill, son, so you can stand on your own. You understand."

"Mom, I can't go back to school. I won't be able to get financial aid and—"

His mother interrupts, "Boy, you are taking these courses, or you can get a job, or get the fuck out of my house! Make your choice, but I ain't playing with you. I'm tired of sitting here and watching you throw your life away to that damn computer. It's time to be a man. I knew I should have married Barry Springfield. He owns his own car wash, and his kids are successful. I'm so disappointed. My family's a damn mess." His mother walks away with a look of disappointment on her face. Past Craig slams his fist before stomping out of the room, leaving us to ourselves.

"Fuck you, Mom! You ruined our lives with your bitterness! You couldn't go a day without drinking, and you never gave a damn about my achievements! Never went to a single game to watch me play! All you cared about was which bottle you were going to drink next. And you wonder why I'm fucked up!" he cries.

Our Craig drops to his knees and breaks down crying. His neck and arms are fully gray. It's now spreading onto his face. His whole body is shaking uncontrollably, and I'm not sure if it's out of sadness or fear. I guess if I were him, I'd be feeling both. If my time comes—which I know it will—I hope it doesn't get this far.

The ball of light flies in the room, then out of the house, once again lighting up the doorway. Craig takes a step and then falls to the floor.

"What's wrong?" Phoenix asks.

"My legs. My legs feel heavier. They're weighing me down," Craig says.

"Come on. Let's help him through," Phoenix says to me. I sigh, throwing one of Craig's arms across my shoulder.

* * *

We walk through the doorway after Daphne and find ourselves in a hospital room.

"I should have known I would end up here. My mom thought she was so smart telling me to go for CNA. It's the worst job ever, and I'm not exaggerating," Craig says.

An old man wearing a disposable gown appears on the hospital bed. The age spots on his pale, wrinkled skin along with snot steadily oozing out of his nose reveal his poor health and hygiene. The former Craig enters the room rolling a cart with a variety of medical and cleaning supplies. He's wearing white scrubs with a black nametag that has his name written in red.

"Okay, it's time to change your diaper. I'm just gonna roll you over," he says while putting on gloves.

Craig rolls him over to his side, revealing his backside. He slowly takes off the man's diaper. The old man begins groaning and coughing. Craig wipes his ass until it's clean. "Almost done," he mutters as he grabs a diaper from the cart. As soon as he turns back around, the old man sneezes. When he does that, he releases feces, spraying out onto Craig's neck and body.

"Oh shit!" I scream, turning around from the sight.

"Literally!" Phoenix yells in surprise.

"Yeah. Literally," Craig says.

"How did you recover from that?" Phoenix asks.

"No, this was it. The final straw. I went to the pawn shop and bought a gun. Then I went home and stared at the gun for what seemed like hours. I worked up the nerve to call Brendon, but he changed his number. I heard he had moved to a different state after all that stuff went down. I just wanted to tell him that I was sorry and that I wasn't myself. I was too late, though," Craig confesses."

I speak. "Well, maybe it's not too late now."

"That it was stupid to kill myself. If I had known I would end up here, I would have had someone else kill me or got into an accident or something," Craig says.

"You probably would have ended up here anyway even if you got someone else to do it, because you're still the cause of your death." Phoenix says.

"Well, I'm done with life. I wasn't good at it. I want to be at peace and do something else," he says somberly.

"So, you're telling me that if you got a second chance to live, you would refuse?" Phoenix asks him.

"I mean yeah, but I never felt right. I was always odd, and nobody understood me. I wanna move on to heaven, but I don't want to live again," Craig says.

"I know I would love to try life again," I say lowly to myself.

"Me too. Life was a cakewalk compared to this place," Phoenix says.

"Speak for yourselves. I said my piece. I did a lot of wrong in my life. I'm sorry I'm a jerk, and I get that now. I just want to rest and forget my life ever existed. I don't fucking care anymore," Craig says.

The doorway lights up again, grabbing our attention. It's brighter than usual, but its energy is giving off a dark vibe. We all walk through the door silently, one by one.

* * *

We arrive right back where we started: Craig's apartment.

"Really? I have to witness this again?" Craig shouts, throwing his hands in the air.

We all watch the former Craig enter his bedroom and sit down on the bed. My stomach drops. Why are we here again? Craig turns on the r&b station and grabs the black box from his bed.

"This is crazy!" Craig says, turning his back on the scene.

Past Craig takes out the gun and points it to his head. He pulls the trigger, and we hear the loud bang. Instead of blood and brains splattering like the first time, there is only ash. His whole body reduces to ashes, leaving a pile where he once sat. We were spared the bloodbath this time.

"Craig, are you okay?" I ask.

I look over at Craig, but he's not there. The others soon notice that he's gone as well. I call his name a few more times. Phoenix runs over to the spot he last stood. He reaches his right arm out to touch the ash, but is blocked by the barrier.

"Where did he go? Where could he be?" Phoenix asks frantically.

"I don't know. He was just here!" I reply.

"Guys, look!" Daphne points toward the bedroom door. We don't see his apartment anymore. We see the void. Did he get sent back to the void? Is that it for him?

Suddenly, a dirt road appears, like the one I ran into when I met the dark ones and Phoenix. Craig appears on the road.

"Craig!" I scream. I run toward the barrier, beating against it, hoping I can get through to him by some miracle. I scream his name again. The others join me, but our efforts are futile.

Craig falls to his knees. He's trying to pick himself back up, but he can't. He lets out the most tortuous scream, which make us beat harder on the barrier. I know it's not helping, but there's nothing else I can do for him. Tears run through my eyes, and all I can do is keep beating.

I watch his clothes rip and his chest grow. He's transforming into a dark one. By now, the spiritual infection had spread across his skin. His eyes are bulging out of his head. Craig grabs his head and bellows in agony. Suddenly, his head starts shaking uncontrollably. Beams of light shoot from his pupils into the sky, and he screams at his highest decibel. He falls to the ground, finally quiet.

A few moments later, he removes himself from the ground. His transformation is complete; he is officially a dark one. He walks down the road as mindlessly as the others. I don't even recognize him anymore. Craig is gone. He's fucking gone.

"Oh, no!" Daphne screams, as tears begin pooling in her eyes.

Phoenix isn't crying, but appears shaken. As for me, I am numb. I knew it was coming. I had a feeling. He still didn't deserve to die. This spiritual nightmare has just gotten real. The rule of nature has always been survival of the fittest. My self-preservation just went from active to overdrive.

"What are we going to do now? What's next? Who's next?" Daphne asks.

"I don't know, Daphne, but we will get through this together. We have to," I say.

"I'm so scared," Daphne cries.

"Good. I'd think you were crazy if you weren't," Phoenix replies.

Suddenly, the whole room goes white, blinding us. I cover my eyes, awaiting what's to come next. I just hope I'm ready.

9

We soon arrive on a bridge. Daylight peeks through the clouds, revealing the world underneath. I walk over to the railing to get a glimpse at the river. The water appears murky, but the current seems strong. It looks unsafe, like the kind of river that has a lot of snakes and fish that bite. I can't imagine anyone swimming in that river.

"I wonder what river this is," I ask in curiosity.

"Like anyone cares about the damn name!" Daphne snaps.

We look at her in surprise. I have never seen her react like that. I know I didn't make the best first impression, but she's got one more time to talk to me like that.

"Daphne, what's wrong? Do you know this place?" Phoenix asks.

Before she could answer, we see her former self appear. She's standing on the railing, balancing herself on a column, looking down at the river. Our Daphne shrieks, covering her hands over her mouth as she does. Blood is dripping down former Daphne's wedding dress, but there are no holes to suggest she has been hurt. Mentally checked out, but not physically hurt. But if she's not hurt, then whose blood is that?

"This is where I died," Daphne says with a shaky tone.

The past Daphne lets go of the railing, falling to her death. We all scream obscenities, caught off guard. It may have seemed obvious that she was about to fall, but to witness it happen was utterly haunting.

"Why did you drown yourself? Why such a painful death?" I ask.

"Because I was hoping for my disappearance to remain a mystery," she answers honestly. That statement sends a chill down my spine.

The ball of light suddenly appears, flying right past us. A wall of light soon follows, traveling past us so gracefully that I couldn't even feel it. As it passes us, the area begins transforming into a different place.

* * *

After the light settles, we look around and find ourselves in an empty restaurant kitchen.

"This is my family's restaurant. I spent most of my life here," Daphne says, crossing her arms.

An overweight man appears, kneeling on the floor. A woman appears soon after, lying beneath him, holding a newborn baby in her arms. Daphne. The new parents are admiring her and planting gentle kisses on her cheeks, giving her an overwhelming amount of affection.

"Oh!" Daphne yelps, placing her hands over her mouth to hold back the sound.

Tears start swelling in her eyes. This must be so painful for her. Her parents seemed to adore her. I never had parents that cared like that, but I imagine that it would suck to leave them behind. That's assuming they lived long enough to see her life play out. Okay, Cadence, try to be empathetic. It's good spiritual points, and you don't want a repeat of Craig.

"I miss you guys so much. I would give anything to just start over. Just to feel flour across my fingertips or smell the bread dough baking. I can still remember the smell. You never forget the smell of home," Daphne confesses in her soft tone.

"No matter how hard you try," I say under my breath.

The ball of light emerges from nowhere, circling around the kitchen. It flies out of the door, causing the doorway to illuminate again. The bright white light flashing before us is mystifying. It sucks you in, almost as if it has its own mild, gravitational pull. I only know that we must walk through it, and we each do, one by one.

* * *

We are led to the front of the restaurant. All the chairs are placed on top of the tables. There is a large, empty pastry case across the entrance, along with a cash register and a long bar table. Right above it, we can see a sign that reads, "Get Your Good Eating at Good Eaton!" I guess that's her family name. That's a clever play on words.

The walls are painted a bright yellow that screams family-friendly and a jukebox that adds a vintage feel. It's your typical bakery, but it's nice, and you can tell a lot of work was put into this place.

Daphne takes the initiative to walk around, observing the place. She walks over to the jukebox and stares at it. She puts her veil over her face in attempt to hide her tears. It's the first time I see her use her veil, and I can't help but feel sympathy for her. She can't hide anymore, though; it's her time to face the music.

Phoenix breaks the silence. "I bet you couldn't stay away from that jukebox? It must have been cool to have."

"We didn't have it for very long. We couldn't keep it," Daphne says.

Suddenly, Daphne's father appears in the room, walking over to the jukebox. He puts in a quarter and presses three buttons. A guitar riff swallows the silence in the air, dominating the room, filling it with a comfortable tension.

"'Time Has Come Today' by The Chamber Brothers. My dad played this song a lot. It really brings back a lot of memories," she says.

Daphne's father walks to the end of the restaurant. We follow him around as he leads us to a single booth. Her mother appears in the booth, holding the toddler version of Daphne. Her father kisses young Daphne on the forehead and pecks his wife on the lips before taking a seat.

Her father begins singing along to the song, word for word. Daphne's mom laughs at her husband's singing before bringing her attention back to younger Daphne.

"She sure is pretty like her mother. I just hope she don't develop my appetite!" Her father laughs wholeheartedly, infecting her mother, causing her symptoms of laughter.

Her father takes a bite of his bagel while he's still laughing. His laughter is soon replaced with coughing and hacking. His right hand reaches for his chest swiftly in reaction to his sudden ailment.

"Honey, what's happening? Are you having a heart attack? Richard, stay with me!" Daphne's mother yells desperately.

He stumbles out of the booth onto the floor, rolling over on his back with his right fist pressed against his chest. Daphne's mother rushes over to him and begins immediate CPR while frantically yelling at him to hang in there for his family. I look over at the booth they were sitting at moments ago, blissfully happy. The younger Daphne is still sitting in the booth watching everything. She looks scared sitting there all alone.

"Richard, come on!" Daphne's mother bellows, beating his chest to get a pulse going. Younger Daphne sees this and begins to cry. The crying quickly escalates to a fit of weeping, and to top it off, the song hasn't ended yet.

We all look over to our Daphne, who hasn't moved a muscle in any area of her body. Her piercing, blue eyes are expressionless. You would think that reliving your father's death would be a painful experience, but she doesn't seem that disturbed by this—either that or she has got a hell of a poker face.

"Do you remember any of this, Daphne?" Phoenix asks.

"Not really. I only remembered the song and that we were having breakfast at the crack of dawn," she replies.

"You're lucky you didn't carry those memories with you, "Phoenix says.

"Yeah, I'm so lucky my dad died before I could read," Daphne snaps back condescendingly.

"I'm not trying to make light of this. I am saying that it would have been even more traumatic if you had held the memory of his death. There's nothing worse than remembering," Phoenix says mournfully, lowering his head as the words leave his lips.

The ball of light appears, zig-zagging around the room, startling us all. It flies out of the restaurant, once again leaving its trace on the doorway. The three of us walk to our next destination of Daphne's twisted life.

* * *

We arrive in an elementary classroom. The classroom is quaint, with the teacher's desk taking up a good portion of the room. There is a generic green chalkboard placed on the wall with a bulletin board hanging on it. The bulletin board has posters of grammatical and scientific facts. The chalkboard has big letters written on it: SHOW AND TELL DAY!

Daphne puts her face in her palms. "This was the worst period of my childhood. My dad was right to worry about me inheriting his appetite. Being around food all the time didn't help that."

An adolescent version of Daphne appears in front of the classroom, catching us by surprise. She is very small and chubby, with a round shape. She has long, light, golden-colored hair braided in a single rope style. The teacher appears behind her, along with students filling up all the previously empty desks. A cart with an electronic Easy Bake Oven appears next to young Daphne. The oven's timer goes off, making a gentle, buzzing noise.

"That means it's done!" young Daphne shouts excitedly. She removes the small dish from the oven and presents it to the class.

"That's how you make chocolate chip cookies with the Easy Bake Oven. It's safe, and my mommy says it's going to prepare me to cook in the big oven someday." younger Daphne says. One of her classmates raises his hand. Younger Daphne gives a warm smile.

"What's your question?" she asks timidly.

The kid answers. "Yeah, did you make enough cookies for all of us?"

"Um...no, I didn't. I'm sorry. It would take a long time to bake cookies for all of you," young Daphne answers.

The kid replies, "So why didn't you ask your mom to bake us some cookies? You knew we would want some. I brought stuff for the class."

"The assignment is called show and tell, not eat and tell. Daphne did an excellent job with her presentation. Now quiet down," the teacher interjects.

Another student speaks out of turn. "She doesn't have any because she's too busy eating them herself. That's why her name is Eaton because she can't stop eating!"

All the children in the classroom begin laughing. The teacher attempts to calm down the students. Younger Daphne angrily throws the cookie dish on the ground and runs out of the classroom, lighting up the door behind her. I guess there isn't any elaborating on this one. We walk through the door again, dreading the next destination.

* * *

We find ourselves back in the kitchen of Daphne's family restaurant. The kitchen looks a bit different. Updated appliances, fresh paint, new shelves stocked full of baker's flour and spices, and a glass office in the corner of the room.

A teenage version of Daphne appears in the office, admiring herself in a full-body mirror. She looks like a different person compared to her current self. This was before she got all her plastic surgery done. She looks stunning; all the weight she had as a child has completely vanished. She looks fit but shapely, dressed in a beautiful rosy pink dress with a sweetheart neckline, decorated with shiny beads.

A peridot necklace with diamond accents drapes her neck, finishing off her outfit perfectly. Her hair is dyed brunette, and curled like waterfalls that reach to the end of her shoulders. Her skin is pale and smooth, glowing like a full moon on a pitch-black night. The only things that aren't different are her eyes—still baby blue, almond-shaped, and hauntingly unforgettable.

"Wait, is that you, Daphne?" Phoenix asks, not believing his eyes himself. Daphne mutters a yes before putting her head down nervously.

"You were beautiful. I mean, you could have passed for a supermodel. Were you in an accident or something?" Phoenix asks.

"No, I was not," she answers curtly.

"Then why would you change your appearance? Because you are perfect here. You were already what most guys wanted and got in great shape. I wish I took you to prom," Phoenix jokes.

Daphne laughs and pats his shoulder, before answering, "Because I didn't have such a sweetheart like you in my life; that's why."

Daphne's mother appears in the room, wearing a chef's uniform, holding a cane in her right hand. She takes off her chef's hat, placing it on the hat rack.

"Hi, mom! My dress just came in; I couldn't wait to get it on. It fits perfect, don't you think?"

"Sweetie, you look amazing. I wish your dad could be here to see you like this. He would be so proud of the beautiful woman you have become," says Daphne's mom.

"Yeah, thanks, Mom. This Friday is going to be the best night of my life. I can't believe how perfect this dress is! The prom theme this year is 'A Night to Remember.' They say the decorations are supposed to be magical." Teenage Daphne does a quick swirl before facing the mirror, fixing her hair.

"Wait, did you say this Friday? That can't be right; I have next Friday. This Friday is the beginning of Passover. The school wouldn't schedule an event on a holiday. That's so slobby and inconsiderate!" Daphne's mom yells, irate. Her blue eyes look ready to bulge out of her face.

"Mom, calm down. You know your blood pressure is already unstable. What's the big deal anyway? A comet will not fall from the sky and destroy humanity as we know it if kids skip out on the first day of Passover. The restaurant will be fine, Mom. For once, can you think about what I want?" Teenage Daphne says.

"No. I don't want to hear it. We have Passover every single year for the Jewish community. How could you not think it would matter? My arthritis is only getting worse, and I need you here. The first day is the most important day; you know that," says Daphne's mom.

"If you are still trying to punish me for wanting to go to an out-of-state college, you can stop now. I'm not going to change my mind. You know not every girl gets asked out by the guy she wanted." Teenage Daphne grabs her things and begins walking out of the room.

"You can be angry, but this place will be yours someday. This is me and your father's gift to you, so you don't have to work like we did. One day, you will understand that," Daphne's mom says, causing Daphne to stop in her tracks.

"I love you, Mom, and I understand all of your sacrifices. I want you to understand too that I am a person with needs and wants different from yours. Only death can keep me from prom, Mom. I am sorry. You can ground me until I graduate; I don't care! I am not missing prom. You can't control me anymore, Mom, and you are going to have to trust that I know what's best for me too." Teenage Daphne walks out of the office, leaving her mother in a disheartened state.

"I'm so sorry, Mom. I miss you. I shouldn't have been so selfish. Maybe things would have been different," says our Daphne.

"I didn't go to prom, if it makes you feel any better. I wanted to, though—so bad. Under your circumstances, I would have gone too," I confess.

Daphne turns to me and says, "Thanks, Cadence."

That's the first time she's said my name. I guess we have finally reached a formal basis with each other. Daphne's mom walks out of the office, lighting the doorway behind her.

10

We walk through the doorway, which is becoming a forced routine. We end up in a college courtyard. It's a beautiful day. The sun is gleaming high in the partly cloudy sky, and flowers are blossoming along the brick pavement laid upon perfectly trimmed green landscape. The green landscape stretches at least a few acres, surrounded by Greco-Roman style buildings.

The courtyard is full of vibrant and active students: a group playing soccer in the distance, friends walking along the brick pavement, jesting and enjoying each other's company. There are also at least a dozen kites in the air, once again making me miss the sensation of the wind.

A few yards away, I notice a bake sale happening. It's hard to miss that large sign with hot pink lettering that reads BAKE SALE. There is a large crowd surrounding it, purchasing items. There are a group of girls wearing identical pink shirts standing behind the booth, working. I notice that Daphne is one of those girls.

"Hey, Daphne, is that you?" I ask, even though I'm sure it's her.

"Yes. I went through an experimental phase," she answers curtly.

I am assuming she is referring to her former self hairstyle. Her hair is dyed burgundy, combed into a neat ponytail that falls past her shoulders. She looks happy here—young, fit, and charismatic. Students are surrounding her, throwing money at her to purchase a pastry. They are losing their minds having to wait in line for their turn. What are they selling, pot pastries?

"My sorority participated in charities every year, and when someone brought up the idea of having a bake sale, I jumped at the opportunity. It was amazing. I brought the girls to my mom's restaurant, and we stayed and baked desserts all night. I showed them how to make homemade cookies, scones, and muffins. I made the cinnamon rolls and cherry pastries because those require skilled hands. We set up the booth and sold it all in record time, as you can see. It made me feel good that people liked my food, and it made them happy to have home-cooked food. We raised a lot of money, and I made so many friends after this event. A lot of great memories," Daphne shares as this piece of her life unfolds before her.

One of the girls sharing the same shirt pushes her way through the crowd, slams a sale's receipt book on the booth, and yells, "We did it, girls! We made our goal!"

All the girls begin jumping up and down excitedly, screaming. They all circle around former Daphne, picking her up and cheering her name. Former Daphne is completely in the moment, laughing and celebrating herself.

I look over to our own Daphne, who is transfixed by the scene. Tears begin to swell in her eyes, and she slightly lifts her veil to her eyes before the first drop falls.

"I wish I could just jump into this memory and relive it one more time. Do it all differently after this point," Daphne confesses.

"I know. We must keep moving forward, though. It's the only way we can overcome it," Phoenix says confidently.

The ball of light appears, flying past us in a spiral-like motion. It flies through the courtyard then into the nearest school building, lighting the doorway.

"This is our cue," Phoenix says. He runs into the building first, passing through the doorway with ease. I'm right behind him, leaving Daphne behind me.

* * *

Once we cross the doorway, we step into a bedroom. The room is designed like a lodge, with its cedar furniture, limestone fireplace, bison taxidermy hanging on the wall, and blue and white Christmas lights dangling from the ceiling, bedazzling the room with its multi-colored beauty. A Hanukkah menorah sits on the bedside table with candles appearing freshly lit. Traditional Hanukkah music is playing softly in the background, which does provide a comfortable, informal atmosphere.

Daphne's mother appears on the bed, lying underneath the covers. She looks very sick; the weight is lost from her much paler face, and her skin is dry and flaking. Her now gray hair has thinned significantly, and the dark circles underneath her weak eyes have deepened beyond repair.

Past Daphne walks into the room with a wine bottle in her hands. She's dressed casually, and her hair is back to its natural blonde color.

"Hi, Mom. I got my diploma framed for you in the living room. I also got your favorite wine," past Daphne says, sitting on the bed next to her mom.

Her mother smiles and sits up. "You are just too wonderful. The Challah bread you made was great. You might want to make more because, well, I swallowed the whole thing."

Past Daphne lets out a wholehearted laugh. "Oh, Mom."

"I'm so sorry I didn't make it to your graduation. I should have taken care of myself better so that I could be there for the important things. I missed your biggest achievement because—"

"Because you're sick," past Daphne interrupts.

"I know. I love you, Daphne, and I know your father would be so proud of you," Daphne's mother confesses.

A solitary tear runs down Daphne's face, and her eyes begin to swell with more. She holds her mother's hands, saying, "I'm so glad you're my mom, and I will always love you." She wipes the tears from her eyes and grabs the wine bottle. "Now it's wine tasting time!" Daphne and her mother laugh together, and she begins to distribute the wine.

"This was the last Hanukah we spent together. She died at the turn of spring," our Daphne admits.

"I'm so sorry," Phoenix says somberly. I softly give my own condolences.

"Me too. I always took her for granted. I always thought she was holding me back, and though she did try, I understand why now. The world is unapologetic and ruthless, and if you're not strong enough, you will die. Like all of us have." Daphne's words haunt the air, crashing into my ears like a tidal wave.

A light appears in the doorway again, catching us by surprise. We walk through hesitantly, completely clueless to what's on the other side.

* * *

We find ourselves back at Daphne's restaurant. The place is packed; every table is filled, and every seat by the bar is taken. It's your typical restaurant environment; everyone eating and enjoying each other's company, some are alone with their laptops, typing away into oblivion or some social network, and some people are even reading the newspaper, which was becoming a pastime when I was alive.

"It was always busy like this. Right after my mom died and I got all the affairs in order, I invested in the restaurant: fresh paint, new seats, and new menus, but our family name, Good Eaton, stayed the same. It was tough keeping a family establishment without a family, though." Daphne speaks as she's observing the scene in retrospection.

We see the former Daphne walking behind the cash register. She stands next to the cashier, directing her attention to a guest.

"Dave. Oh, Dave." As our Daphne speaks, her words convey a somber tone. I assume that Dave is the guest that past Daphne is speaking to.

"Who was he to you?" I ask curiously.

"He was my husband," Daphne answers curtly.

I walk closer to the scene, with Phoenix close behind. Daphne stays put, but continues to watch the scene.

We hear the cashier speak. "He was just wanting to know if he could put his flier on our bulletin board."

Dave interjects. "Excuse me. My name is Dr. McRight. I just opened my practice a couple of buildings down. I figured—"

Former Daphne retorts, "You want to advertise your business. What type of doctor are you, a general practitioner?"

"No. I practice general dentistry. A sweet tooth is a sick tooth." Dave laughs at himself, and you can see his perfectly arched, pearly white smile. Past Daphne seems taken aback, blushing and acting in a shy manner.

"Well yes, you have my full permission. Thank you for consulting us first. You're welcome anytime," says past Daphne.

Dave brings out his hand for her to shake. She grabs it confidently, asserting herself.

Dave speaks. "Wow, I have never met a business owner as...young as you are. You must be a very motivated and determined person."

"Well, it takes one to know one. Good luck with your business, Dr..."

"Dr. McRight. But you can call me Dave. I didn't catch your name," he says, smile stretching from ear to ear.

"I'm Ms. Eaton. Good luck, Dave. Thanks for stopping by."

Past Daphne begins to turn and walk away before hearing Dave say, "Thank you, Ms. Eaton. True luck would be winning a date with you."

"I wouldn't hold your breath," past Daphne says as she begins to walk away.

Dave laughs to himself before collecting his briefcase and walking out of the restaurant, lighting up the doorway as he does.

I look over at our Daphne, and she has her back turned to the scene. I walk over to her to see if she is okay. She looks a little displaced, but she isn't crying.

I speak softly. "Hey, Daphne, it's time to go. The door is lit."

She walks toward the door with her eyes stuck on the ground, without saying a word. I look at Phoenix, and he just throws his hands in the air like he's not getting involved. We walk through the doorway into the next destination.

* * *

I walk through looking at my feet, and I notice we're standing on red leaves. My eyes follow the leaves until they lead to past Daphne and Dave getting married. People are clapping, and we can see the bride and groom kissing, concluding the ceremony.

This wedding is almost mystical with its fall theme. There are trees on the end of each aisle with leaves painted in autumn colors. There are lanterns everywhere with lit candles. Daphne looks radiant and full of happiness in Dave's arms. It's the wedding of any girl's dreams; the bride and groom are both beautiful and happy, and everyone around them is celebrating their union.

Her wedding dress looks flawless, and her hair is braided in a stylish bun topped with that perfectly matched veil. Our Daphne seems resentful when asked about her husband now, but they seemed to have had a positive start. I look over at our Daphne, and this time, she can't fight back the tears in her eyes. Phoenix seems to have noticed too, as he walks over to console her.

"This was a beautiful moment. You were so beautiful," Phoenix says.

She wipes her eyes and clears her throat before replying," Yeah, a beautiful lie."

The bride and groom begin to walk down the aisle hand in hand, ready to celebrate their commitment. Our Daphne looks at the scene, shaking her head.

"If only I knew," Daphne says somberly.

I look at my own ring finger, trying to picture the once beautiful sapphire ring that decorated it. I can't imagine how I'm going to feel when I see my fiancé. How we dared to rise before our inevitable fall. Despite everything, I still see his face whenever I close my eyes, as if he never left me. I know the truth, though; I know I will never see my love again, and that is what hurts the most. The one thing I was running away from is what I now miss the most.

The doorway lights up as the bride and groom exit the wedding event. Daphne walks through without hesitation, as the scene appears to be causing her stress. If everything changed from this point, then what can we expect? What did her husband do to her to make her regretful? I know the answers will be revealed in due time, but there are so many terrible scenarios that I can't help but wonder.

"One door at a time," Phoenix says, walking through. I soon follow into the next chapter of Daphne's life story.

11

We find ourselves back in Daphne's restaurant. The place is empty, suggesting that the establishment is closed. The chairs on the tables are a dead giveaway. I see the former Daphne sitting at a booth, signing paperwork with an older Hispanic woman.

Our Daphne runs toward them, shouting, "No! Stop! Don't sign it! Just don't!"

She begins beating on the invisible barrier. I didn't expect such a strong reaction from such a seemingly boring memory. I just stand there, watching her freak out. Phoenix rushes over to stop her. She begins crying and buries herself into his chest. He just stands there hugging her awkwardly.

So, I ask her, "Why would you sell your family's restaurant if it means so much to you?"

She stops sobbing, silencing herself before raising her head from Phoenix's chest to answer, "Because I thought I didn't need it anymore. After I got married,

Dave asked me if I could help him with his accounting issues because his business had a rough start. I also helped him with better advertising, and we eventually got great clients. Clients with power and money rolled in quickly. I couldn't both run my business and keep his on track, so I made the sacrifice. I sold it to my mother's best friend, Rosa. I believed she would take care of it the way my mother intended. Things sometimes don't work out the way you want them to. I wish I had thought it through more."

Daphne removes herself from Phoenix, facing the opposite direction from us. The doorway then lights up, signaling us to walk through. Phoenix guides Daphne through the doorway gently, like he's walking on eggshells. I hang back and watch them pass through. I take a deep breath, closing my eyes before following.

$$* * *$$

I open my eyes to see a grieving Daphne, not crying anymore, but eyes developing fresh tears. Phoenix looks a little exasperated, and here I am: just here. I look around and notice that we are in an office. I'm assuming this is her husband's practice.

The former Daphne appears in the office chair, typing on her computer. She still looks very beautiful and youthful, and her blonde hair is shiny and thick, combed into a perfect bun. Dave walks into the room wearing his lab coat over his professional attire.

"Hi, sweetheart. Do you have a minute to greet the new hire?" Dave asks politely.

"You already decided? I thought we were going to choose together?" past Daphne says, turning around from her seat to face him.

"I know, but you have been working so hard, I didn't want you to worry. Vickie, come on in," says Dave.

An alluring young woman walks into the room. She is in her early twenties, with a petite figure and curly, blonde hair that reached her shoulders. She looks like she should be a beauty pageant participant, not cleaning teeth. I would never in my life have a woman like that work closely with my husband. Fuck that. I wonder how Daphne handled this.

"Honey, this is Vickie. She is our new dental assistant," Dave says nonchalantly.

"So, she will be working with you?" Daphne asks, standing up from her chair with a slightly worrisome expression.

"She will be working with all of the doctors, including me. She has just been certified, and I think she's going to fit right in, sweetheart." Dave walks over to Daphne and kisses her on the head.

"I'm quite impressed and grateful for the opportunity to work with you, Daphne," says Vickie confidently.

"It's Mrs. McRight. I'm glad to meet you, Vickie, and I'm looking forward to seeing you at work," Daphne says, giving her a forced smile.

"I guess I will see you next week. Thank you again for the opportunity," says Vickie.

"Thank you. We'll see you soon," says Dave.

Vickie exits the room. Daphne lightly slaps Dave on the shoulder.

"Are you serious? She looks like she's barely old enough to drink, and she's looks like that! Do you not find that tempting?" Daphne inquires.

"What? No, of course not. You're my wife! I prefer inexperienced assistants because they are easier to train. Older women are hard to work with; you can't teach an old dog new tricks. Besides, she's engaged. I met her fiancé today; he was a nice guy. He's sitting in the lobby waiting for her now. She's taken, so you have nothing to worry about. It's not temptation, honey, it's business, and a girl like her will have clients wanting to come back for anything. Trust me: this is a good business decision," Dave answers.

Dave hugs her from behind, swaying her in a side to side motion before nibbling on one of her ears. She giggles like a school girl, and they share a deep kiss.

"It was a terrible business decision. I should have never believed that lie. Maybe I wouldn't have lived one," Daphne says.

"He cheated on you with her?" Phoenix asks quizzically.

Daphne turns to him and says, "He did a lot of things he shouldn't have."

The office door lights up, and Daphne instantly walks through. Phoenix walks through next, brushing his hair from his face as he does. This experience is starting to take its toll. I don't think I'm far behind him in that sense. I force myself through the doorway, reminding myself that each door brings me closer to my resolution—to all of ours, hopefully. I really do hope so. I don't know if I can deal with everyone else turning into a dark one and erasing themselves from existence—more importantly, my own existence.

* * *

I cross through, stepping onto a sandy beach on a bright and beautiful day. The ocean waves overlap one another, landing gracefully onto shore. There are children running around, playing on shore and chasing seagulls. The beach is filled with people. I see guys surfing in the distance and others riding in speedboats, and they all seem to be having a great time. Some people are tanning on the beach, while others lay themselves under beach umbrellas. Nothing out of the ordinary; just a normal day at the beach.

"It's weird how we're on a beach, and we can't smell the ocean breeze or feel the sand on our feet," Phoenix says.

"I could never forget the smell," Daphne says.

Past Daphne appears in front of us, lying on a lawn chair with Dave under a beach umbrella. They both look picture perfect in their bathing suits with matching, luxurious sunglasses. A young woman in a red bikini walks past them as if she's doing a catwalk down a runway, begging to be seen. Dave lowers his sunglasses, checking her out as she walks by.

"Geez, Dave. Close your mouth; you're drooling. Way to kill our honeymoon phase, murderer," younger Daphne says, running a finger through her blonde hair.

"Oh, come on. You can't be serious? That girl is nothing next to you," Dave says defensively.

"So why did she take your attention away from me? I'm sitting right next to you, and you have the nerve to drool over another woman walking by. What's wrong with you?" past Daphne snaps.

"Where is all this coming from? You're my wife— my number one. Why do you have to be so insecure?" Dave asks.

"Well, checking out other women on the market with blatant disregard for your wife doesn't help anyone's insecurities, except for the other woman. You wouldn't like it if I checked out a guy you thought was attractive right in front of you."

"Okay, fine. I'm sorry. I didn't mean to upset you. I always want to keep you happy. You are so perfect when you're happy," Dave says as he caresses her cheek.

"After my surgery, I'll always be perfect," Daphne says confidently. She repositions herself in her chair and relaxes, remaining silent along with Dave.

"Guys!" I yell, seeing the ball of light flying around us.

It shoots off like a bullet as it's flying toward the ocean. The light travels a few hundred feet offshore until it reaches the deep end and dives in the water.

"I'm so sick of swimming!" Daphne yells.

I can't help but agree mentally, but I don't have to remind her that there are no other options. We all run into the ocean until we can't feel the floor, and we're floating. The water begins spinning, creating a whirlpool like the one that transported us here. I hold my breath and surrender myself to the pull. The only choice I have is to be a willing passenger when I'm at the mercy of a force I don't understand. We all sink under, falling into blackness once more.

* * *

I awaken with the others, standing in a doctor's office. We can see the former Daphne sitting on an exam bed. Her nose is bandaged up, and she's wearing a post-op surgical bra and blue leggings. Her breasts are at least a DD size, if I had to guess—at least twice the size they were before. She's sitting upright, facing the mirror mounted on the wall. She then closes her eyes and begins rubbing her temples, humming as she does it.

I wonder if this is her first surgery. I look over to our Daphne, and she is immersed with the scene. Phoenix is also engaged. I think he is secretly hoping he gets to see a pair of breasts. Although, if you ask me, we've seen more of Daphne than we already should have. I feel very uncomfortable but like any itch you can't scratch you have to wait for it to pass.

The doctor walks into the room and takes a seat in front of past Daphne. She immediately directs her attention toward him. He begins the conversation by saying, "Hello, Mrs. McRight. Today is the big day. Now, your nose is still healing, but your breasts should be ready to play. Please remove your bra, and we'll get started."

Past Daphne steps off the exam bed and removes her bra, throwing it where she was previously sitting. The doctor begins examining her breasts.

"Tell me if anything hurts, okay," says the doctor.

He presses his fingers against her breasts and massages them in a circular motion until his hands have touched around each. She has her eyes closed as he does this, appearing as calm as a dove swimming on a quiet sunny day.

"Okay, you feel great. You look fantastic. How does everything feel to you?" the doctor asks.

She turns toward the mirror on the wall, observing her breasts. They aren't as big as our Daphne's, which tells me she went back for round two at some point. They are significantly bigger, though. Past Daphne smiles as she checks herself out in the mirror. "Everything feels perfect," she exclaims.

"Well, that's what I want to hear. I think your husband will be very happy with the results, and he's a very lucky man. Most men don't have a woman who cherishes her appearance. If you want to keep shooting for perfection, you know who to call. I'm going to fill out your paperwork, Mrs. McRight, and one of our nurses will take care of everything else. Ask any questions, and you will be taken care of."

The doctor begins to walk out of the room before past Daphne says, "Daphne!"

"Excuse me?" the doctor asks, giving his attention to her.

"Call me Daphne, please. Once you touch a woman's breasts, you are well past formalities."

The doctor laughs wholeheartedly before saying, "Thank you, Daphne. Anything you need, you just ask."

He walks out of the room, leaving Daphne to herself. She turns back toward the mirror admiring her brand new breasts.

"Was this the first surgery?" I ask our Daphne.

"The first of many," she answers. "I remember that day like it was yesterday. I thought all my problems had been solved. I thought that if I had the perfect body, my husband would never desire another woman. I was more beautiful than I had ever been. That was supposed to be enough."

"You would have been plenty for me," Phoenix says out of the blue. His eyes are still glued to past Daphne's breasts.

Our Daphne crosses her arms, looking down to hide her wide grin. The office doorway lights up, indicating that our time is up, and our next destination is underway.

I speak. "Guys, it's time to go."

Daphne leaves first, taking one more look before she does. I begin walking, but I notice that Phoenix is nowhere close. I turn around to see him still staring at the former Daphne. His hands are pressed against the barrier, and he looks deep in thought.

"Hey, you have to switch back to your big head sometime!" I yell at him before walking through.

* * *

Phoenix starts walking the second I step through. I turn my attention to him, and he says to me, "Sorry, I don't know if I'm gonna get a view like that again."

I smile and say, "Nothing to apologize for. Just keeping you in check."

We smile at each other before turning our attention to the scene. We are back in her husband's dental practice. The street lights peak through the blinds of this closed establishment.

The former Daphne appears at the front entrance, unlocking the door and letting herself inside. She walks over to the front desk and retrieves a cell phone. It appears to be cold out, as she is dressed in a long, flashy fur coat with stylish snow boots. I look over at our Daphne, and she has the look of fury on her face. This is not a good flashback.

Suddenly, we hear glass break in the back room. A woman begins giggling, and is suddenly silenced. Former Daphne follows the sound, and we are all practically glued behind her. She stops in front of her husband's office, and slowly opens the door. We follow her into the office, and I gasp in shock at what I see. Phoenix mutters a curse word, and our Daphne can barely stand to look. Once was bad enough.

Vickie is on top of Dave's desk wearing only an opened blouse, breasts completely exposed, with Dave cupping his hand over one of them. His other hand is down her Area 51, where no married man is ever supposed to be. Past Daphne drops her jaw and everything in her hands onto the ground. This gets the attention of Vickie.

"Daphne!" Vickie quickly jumps off the desk and begins getting dressed and collecting her things.

"It's Mrs. McRight, you shameless whore!" past Daphne yells.

Dave quickly rises, zipping his pants up and trying to put himself back together. "Honey, please don't do anything rash. We'll...figure this out."

"You are fired, bitch! If you don't get out of my sight in five seconds, I will make sure no one will ever see your whore face again! You are done! Done, bitch!" she yells with a sharpness that cuts the bone.

Daphne picks up a floor lamp standing next to her and lunges it at Vickie, hitting her legs. Vickie falls to the ground, screaming, before getting up and running out of the office. Daphne turns to Dave, and they have a momentary stare down.

"How could you?" she gasps as tears fall effortlessly down her face.

"I'm sorry," Dave says, looking down on the floor in contempt.

"No, I need more than sorry. You tell me why! Everything that I sacrificed for this business and our future, and you do this!" Daphne screams.

Her face is blood red, and her bottom lip is quivering from all the crying. I notice that her lips are different. They are fuller, like they are in the present. Her nose looks noticeably slimmer and pointy, and her skin has started aging. She's changed a lot since we saw her first surgery. Here is where her downward spiral began.

"Okay, you want an explanation? I'll give you one. You spend more time on yourself than you do with me anymore. Ever since you started this cosmetic surgery craze, our sex life has suffered. You spend weeks at a time recovering from surgeries, and by the time you're healed, you have to get your nails done, or a tan, or some other stupid beauty regime. Oh, not to mention the money you spend on all these things!" Dave yells, slapping a coffee mug off his desk.

"How dare you? I deserve everything I get. I have worked hard, and we have an image to upkeep. I don't see how that merits you to stick your hand down another woman's vagina!" Daphne screams.

"This isn't want I signed up for. I don't even recognize you anymore. You're not the woman I married," Dave utters, as if he's given up on the conversation.

"Yes, I am the woman you married! I am Daphne Eaton, no matter what I change! You're supposed to look me in the eyes and see that!" Daphne says.

Dave walks up to her, his blue eyes staring fiercely into hers, and says, "How am I supposed to love you when you don't even love yourself?"

Daphne pauses at his comment and gives him a look that could kill. She speaks. "Without me, you would be nothing! You couldn't run a business if it grew on your ass! I saved you! Who brought you clients? Me! Who reorganized your entire staff and made you so much money that we even have this lifestyle? Me! You just have the—"

"The what?" Dave interjects. "The skills! The skills that I went to school for eight years to get and used to start a business of my own. You helped, but you invested no money into my business, just your time. Don't you dare try to take credit for all my success! I am sorry; this is bad. I really feel horrible that you had to find out like this, but you need to calm down. Yelling at each other won't solve anything, and I will do anything you say to make this as right as I can. I am so sorry, Daphne. I NEVER meant for this to happen."

"You know, I could have left you for my plastic surgeon. He's in love with me, but I never slept with him because I respect our marriage. Because he's my surgeon, he gets to touch me wherever he wants, and I let him. I would close my eyes and feel his hands admire my beauty, knowing that if I had said one word, he could have been mine," Daphne confesses coldly.

"Oh, okay. So that's why you're so addicted to plastic surgery! Why you always plan the next one before you have even healed from your post-op. Okay, well Daphne, it's like you said: you deserve everything you get."

"I hope you get set on fire!" Daphne screams before stomping out of the office, crying. The doorway lights up behind her.

"I'm so sorry, Daphne," I say sympathetically.

She looks at me and says, "So am I."

Our Daphne follows her past self of the office and through the light. Phoenix quietly walks through next with a dismal look on his face. I'm close behind, walking through the light, not guessing where I'm going next. I'm just riding this chaotic memory train.

12

We arrive inside a different office. The office is very professional, set at the top floor with a spectacular view of the city. The sun shines brightly on a baby blue, clear sky. There is a long, marble desk that takes up half the space in the entire room, and there is the former Daphne sitting across from her husband.

Two men in typical professional attire walk into the room, and each take a seat next to them both. This scene has divorce written all over it. Dave looks stressed out and has developed gray streaks in his hair. Daphne looks exactly as we know her now: furiously depressed.

Dave's lawyer speaks first. "Okay, Daphne, we are just going to go through the arrangements once more and make sure both parties agree. If both of you agree—and I hope you do—then you both will sign the divorce papers, and this is all over. Today's the day you guys can move forward with your lives if everyone can keep a level head. Now Daphne, Mr. McRight wants to give you everything you want. He will pay you a five-million-dollar settlement along with $10,000 monthly spousal support. You can also have the property in Jamaica, and he is also willing to buy back your old business or fund a new one in your name. All my client wants in return is to keep the house he has paid for in full and his business that he invested in himself. Do you have any questions, Ms. Eaton?"

"Excuse me. I am not Ms. Eaton until I sign the papers, and nothing will be signed because I am not satisfied. The business is just as much mine as his. There would be no business if it weren't for me!" she exclaims.

"Here we go again," Dave says, covering his hand over his face in frustration.

"Daphne, this is the best deal you are going to get," her lawyer says. "Legally, his business is his because he never signed anything over to you. You have no rights to his business. You're getting a lot more than what most wives get."

"Most wives aren't me!" Daphne yells.

"Daphne, listen. I'm trying to make this easy for us. I'm giving you what you want. I am trying hard to make this right. You have money and plenty of time to fix yourself up, find a new husband, and start over. I want you to be happy and to love life again. This is the first step toward doing that for both of us," Dave pleads.

"That's easy for you to say; you have someone to go to at night. You're replacing me with that bitch who doesn't even know you. She will never love you like I did or take care of you the way I did. You are bent if you think I'm going to let you move on and live happily ever after with her after everything I gave up," former Daphne retorts.

"I don't love you, Daphne. Not anymore. I am happy with another woman. You can hate me, curse me, and even try to sabotage me, but it happened, and it will never change. How I feel will never change. I am done with your petty games and you sitting here like you played no influence in all of this! You have to accept what is and deal with it! I'm expecting soon; I have the weight of the world on me right now!" Dave begins panting, and he quickly pops a Valium in his mouth and pours himself a glass of water.

"Expecting?" she says in shock.

Tears fill her eyes rapidly, and she covers her mouth to keep from bursting into tears. She runs out of the office without saying a word. Her lawyer calls after her, but Dave begs him to let her leave.

The room is suddenly empty, leaving us all alone to deal with it. I was hoping to see the doorway light up, but it doesn't. I look over at our Daphne, whose face is completely emotionless. She looks checked out from all of this. Phoenix walks over to her and speaks. "Hey, I know this is hard. That divorce wasn't on you; it was on him. He made a vow to you and broke it. He wasn't the one for you."

"I just feel so duped. How did I not see what a bastard he was? How ungrateful and fucking selfish he was. I just couldn't let him get away with it. I wasn't going to let him have his happiness while I hid away in Jamaica, wasting my life away," Daphne says, turning away from us.

"But you wasted your life anyway. We all did," I say in conflict with her logic.

"You don't know how it feels to watch your husband choose someone else over you and start a new life. I wanted a family! I gave him everything! He deserved everything he got!" our Daphne yells.

The office doorway suddenly lights up, catching us off guard. Daphne storms off first, walking through the doorway with an attitude.

I look over to Phoenix and ask, "What are we about to witness?"

"I have no idea. I'm not sure I'm ready to go through," he answers.

"I don't want to go through either. Whatever happens to Daphne, one of us will be next, to lead this mind-bending, spiritually retrospective fucking maze that we're in! What if there is no peace in the end, and all of this is in vain?" I speak worriedly.

"There is peace. Come on, Cadence. You were the one who convinced me of that. Don't let the fear get to you. We're getting too close," Phoenix says. He pulls me into a hug and speaks again. "We're in this together, remember?"

"We're stuck together," I reply bitterly.

He lets me go and places his hand at the center of my back, gently propelling me forward. We walk through the doorway into another page of Daphne's life.

* * *

I see our Daphne watching her former self, who is wearing the same wedding dress, but without the blood stains. She is at the front door of a mansion, looking around for something. She looks very determined to find what she's seeking.

"I couldn't take hearing those words in my head. When Dave said he was expecting, I finally broke. It played in my head like a broken record until I couldn't take it anymore. What little sanity that was left in me had escaped the moment he said those words." our Daphne says softly, but void of feelings.

Past Daphne lifts a Buddha statue, revealing a house key. She quietly grabs it and quickly lets herself inside. Phoenix and I follow her with our Daphne close behind. Past Daphne walks into the living room. She looks at all the picture frames and notices that they have all been replaced with Dave's baby mama. She shakes her head profusely and lifts her dress up to remove a pistol from her holster.

"Oh, shit!" I say aloud. She's actually doing this. Am I about to see what I think I'm about to see?

Former Daphne turns to walk upstairs before bumping into a baby stroller, making a slight noise. She kicks the stroller out of her way furiously and walks upstairs, holding her pistol with purpose.

We are all following, watching her every move. She quietly walks up to the bedroom door, which is slightly ajar, and slowly pushes it wide open, preventing as much noise as possible. She walks into the bedroom and stands right in front of the bed where Dave and Vickie are sleeping soundly.

She puts her hands behind her back, concealing her weapon. She walks over to the door and slams it shut, causing both Dave and Vickie to jump awake from their sleep.

"What the hell?" Dave shouts, turning on the lamp on his nightstand. "Daphne, what the fuck are you doing here? This is the craziest thing you've ever done!"

"Dave, get her out of my house. This is so disturbing!" Vickie shouts.

"I'm calling the police. I'm not dealing with this," Dave says.

Daphne shoots the phone as he's reaching for it, shattering his chance to call for help.

"Shit!" Dave screams in shock. Vickie screams too, and they are both completely horrified. Daphne has gotten their full attention now.

"No, Dave. You have to accept what is and deal with it. Isn't that what you told me?" Daphne says, smiling condescendingly.

"Daphne, this is crazy. You have lost it this time. If you stop this now, I promise I won't call the cops. You're not going to shoot us. It would be stupid. You would lose everything, and for what? For revenge? And why are you wearing that damn dress. It's pathetic. Put the damn gun down! I've had it with you!"

Dave attempts to move from the bed, and Daphne fires a shot at him, piercing him through his shoulder. She gasps as she shoots him, eyes filled with a look of exhilaration.

I cover my mouth with both hands in shock, witnessing this act. Phoenix has his arms crossed with a disturbed look on his face. I notice him scoot closer to me and away from our Daphne. Our Daphne is watching the scene in a very cold, unfazed manner. I turn back to this real-life horror scene, engaged and completely terrified.

"Please don't do this. I'm pregnant with his child; you can't kill a child," Vickie begs.

"You're pregnant by another woman's husband! You know, once upon a time, people used to stone women like you. Harlot." Past Daphne speaks coldly.

Dave lunges at Daphne, but he's too far away, giving her enough time to shoot him in the chest. The loud bang is deafening, and I jump back in fear. I feel Phoenix's hands grab my shoulders, but he doesn't take his eyes off the scene.

Past Daphne looks at Dave lying on the ground, his blood splattered all over her dress and onto him. He has a hole the size of a marble ball in his chest. He's coughing up blood, dying painfully.

"No, you're not dying yet, you son of a bitch!" Daphne says. She walks over to Vickie and grabs her hair, yanking her over to Dave. She's crying and pleading for her life, holding her hands in the air.

Daphne drops her to her knees next to Dave and points the pistol at the back of her head.

Still crying, Vickie grabs Dave's hand and says, "I love you, Dave—no matter what. We're going to be together again. It's okay."

Daphne gets enraged at this and screams her heart out before releasing another bullet from the chamber, shooting Vickie in the back of the head. Dave tries to scream, but can only cough up more blood. You can see the tears running down his eyes as he squeezes Vickie's dead hand one more time before dying himself, both hand in hand.

Blood, bits of brain matter, and bone are drenched all over Daphne, and she looks terrifying. "The Bride of Nightmares" is what I would call her if this were a movie. That's what scares me the most, is that this really happened. She was capable of all these things. Her husband was an asshole and so was Vickie, but they didn't deserve to die. They didn't deserve this. No one does.

Former Daphne coldly drops her weapon on the floor and walks out of the room, lighting up the doorway behind her.

"How could you do this?" I screech, not realizing that I'm crying myself.

"They deserved it! They deserve what they got!" our Daphne screams.

"She was pregnant! You killed a mother and her child. You're a monster! They didn't deserve to die, Daphne! You don't get to decide that!" I yell in defense.

"You don't get to judge me, bitch. We're both in here!" Daphne shouts back.

"No, Daphne. You need to hear it!" Phoenix speaks up. "You killed innocent people. They may have wronged you, but they didn't deserve to be murdered in cold blood. You can't sit here and tell me you don't feel any remorse for what the fuck we just saw. I've never seen anybody be that cold and calculated. You're better than this, Daphne. I've been here with you. You can see the wrong in this; I know it."

Our Daphne turns toward the doorway, getting ready to walk through.

She stops when I say, "You can't run away, Daphne; it's now or never! If you don't face them and say you're sorry, you'll end up just like Craig. I'm really trying to help, Daphne. We both want you to find peace and be happy."

The ghostly forms of Dave and Vickie appear in front of Daphne. They are holding hands, and they look at her in sorrow. Daphne turns around and looks at us with tears filling her eyes.

"I know I was wrong, okay? I know I'm a murderer. I shouldn't have done that." Daphne turns back around toward the ghosts and says, "But I can never forgive them. I won't."

"Daphne, wait. Please," Phoenix pleads, but she walks away, ignoring him.

Daphne walks through the doorway, stomping through the ghosts with blatant disregard. They turn around, giving Daphne, an afflicted look before disappearing. Phoenix and I give each other a worried look before walking through ourselves.

* * *

We arrive back at the bridge where Daphne died. She is standing behind her old self, watching her balance on the rails, preparing to jump.

"Daphne!" I yell for her attention. Phoenix and I walk up to her, and I touch her shoulder, but her dress falls to the ground and somehow, her body vanishes into thin air.

I look up and see old Daphne still standing on the rail. She turns her head, we see her face, and I scream in shock. Daphne's old self is a dark one; her face is gray, and she has no irises. Daphne is gone.

She lets go of the rails, falling off the bridge to her death. Phoenix and I rush toward the rails, but it's too little too late as we watch Daphne fall into the river. We scream out and attempt to reach for her, but she keeps falling until she hits the water. I watch her come up from the river, and the water turns blood red, revealing other dark ones. A school of soulless creatures are swimming in a river of death, where the truly damned go.

Phoenix pulls me from the rails, and I fall into his chest, sobbing uncontrollably. I just let it all go. Phoenix holds onto me, but I know he's crying too. All we have is each other with no glimmer of hope, and one of us is next.

I fall to the ground with Phoenix still holding onto me, and we both just sit there. A few minutes pass by, and I find myself still crying. My sobbing begins to slow down, and my breathing begins to relax. I don't even notice the yawns passing through my lips between all the quivering, but that doesn't stop sleep from taking over me.

I feel my eyelids falling and my head drop, and before I know it, I have successfully cried myself to sleep. One thing I know for sure now is that I'll wake up. I'll wake up in a new chapter of either one of our lives. I'm far from ready to face myself, but unfortunately, life continues whether you cooperate or not. That fact has just been proven to me once again.

13

I feel a heavy hand pressing on my shoulder, and I jolt right awake. I am greeted by Phoenix's face as he's crouching over me to make sure I'm okay. He helps me up from the ground, and I take a second to straighten up my nightgown. I begin observing the room, realizing that we're in the next place. It's a garage with boxes packed everywhere and tools hanging on the wall. I don't recognize this place at all.

I look at Phoenix, and he appears to be distressed. No, it's more than that; he's scared, which tells me this is his turn. This is the first time I've seen him afraid, although his fear is justified.

I ask, "Do you remember how we got here?"

"No, I don't. I dozed off shortly after you, and I woke up here. I've been trying to wake you for a few minutes now, and I'm glad I succeeded because I know exactly what memory this is," Phoenix reveals.

A vintage, black Camaro surfaces in the center of the room. Phoenix jumps back in surprise, muttering curse words under his breath. The windows are tinted, but there's enough clarity to see the former Phoenix sitting in the driver's seat, drinking alcohol and smoking a cigar.

I notice that all the windows are raised up except one. One window in the back seat is slightly open, fitting a hose that extends to the exhaust pipe. The ignition starts, and smoke begins to fill the car. I see past Phoenix slouch back into his seat and fall asleep to his death.

"It seemed like the best way to go out. I didn't feel any physical pain, and before I knew it, I fell asleep. Now here I am. If only I had known I was going to end up right back here."

"If only. Your death was more graceful than mine. At least you thought it through. I acted out of impulse. If you don't mind me asking, what year Camaro is that?" I say curiously, redirecting the subject matter.

Phoenix chuckles before answering. "It's a 1960 make. It belonged to my maternal grandfather, who passed it to my mom. It's the only possession I had left from her, other than a family picture I kept in my wallet."

The garage door lifts, exposing a bright light in front of us. We give each other a quick glance before walking through, entering the next destination.

We find ourselves in a hospital room. Right in front of us is a mother holding her newborn baby, and the father standing right above.

"Mom. It's really her," Phoenix says, walking straight up to her. He tries to touch her face, but the barrier prevents him. His mom is humming a sweet melody while his father is admiring them both. He looks like any happy father you'd expect. The quintessential picture-perfect parents and their perfect newborn son.

Phoenix's eyes are bloodshot from crying, but not a single tear has yet to fall.

"Can you believe we made him? He's going to be a football player; look at his shoulders!" his dad says in excitement.

His mother replies, "I don't care what he does; he's now my sweet boy forever and ever." She kisses baby Phoenix on the cheek. His father kisses his wife on top of the head, and they continue to marvel at their baby boy.

"I can't believe I got to see her again. She was taken from me too soon. She looks so beautiful here. I forgot how happy my dad used to be with my mom.

They really did love each other," Phoenix says, reminiscing.

"They loved you too. You guys were the perfect family," I say in this emotional moment.

"Yeah, then why didn't we get the perfect life?" Phoenix asks bitterly.

The hospital doorway lights up, signaling us to move forward. Phoenix takes one more look at his family before walking through in haste without saying a word. He's obviously very upset by all of this. I can give him space, and when he needs someone to fall on, I will be there. I owe him that for saving me and helping me along the way. Phoenix will find peace, or I will die again trying. We will both find peace. It's not all over yet, and we still have a chance. I take my step through, this time with purpose.

* * *

I step onto a small cliff next to a beautiful, sky blue lake. The unruffled water is inviting and calm. I see Phoenix standing near the edge of the cliff, looking down at the water. I walk up to him and glance over the cliff to see his mother backstroking carelessly in the water. She swam like a swan—gliding across the water with effortless grace and power.

"This was my mom's favorite place, I believe. We camped here at least twice a year, and it was always so much fun. She was always teaching me things, and every time she spoke, her voice always resonated with me," Phoenix confesses.

A kid resembling Phoenix emerges in front of us. He must be between eight and ten years of age here. He's standing on the edge of the cliff with a worried expression stamped on his face. He suddenly drops down, hugs his knees, and begins quivering.

"Mom, I can't jump. I'm too scared! It's too high!"

"Sweetie, if it was too high, I wouldn't let you jump at all. It looks high because you're looking down, but I promise this cliff is as tall as me. You dove higher than that before many times," his mother replies.

"But I was in a pool; real water is scary. What if there is an anaconda in there?" young Phoenix cries.

His mother giggles at his question before answering, "Sweetie, the only anacondas in America are inside museums. Anacondas come from South America, but there are no snakes at all. I promise. Look how clear and beautiful the water is. You see how free-flowing it is? That's how you know it's good to swim in. Look at me; I'm having a blast!" his mother says as she's floating with ease.

"I'm still scared," says little Phoenix.

"Then that's exactly why you should jump. Sweetheart, life is going to throw so many things at you, sometimes all at once. You can't let fear hold you back from what you're meant to do. Besides, you want to be an Eagle Scout someday, right?" his mother asks.

"I'm already an Eagle Scout!" The younger Phoenix flexes his arms as he says this, causing his mother to laugh.

"Well, Eagle Scout, are you fearless?" she asks.

"Yes. I am fearless," little Phoenix says.

"Prove it, and jump, my little Eagle Scout!" his mom yells.

Little Phoenix jumps from the cliff, screaming at the top of his lungs. He dives feet first into the lake, landing close to his mother. She screams in excitement and helps him reach the surface. She gives him a big hug, and I can vaguely hear her say, "I'm so proud of my Eagle Scout."

Little Phoenix shouts, "I wanna go again; that was awesome!"

"I wish I had that," I reveal somberly.

"I wish everyone had this. Maybe the world would've been less fucked up. I don't think I ever thanked her for loving me unconditionally," Phoenix admits.

His words sting as they travel through my ears, and my eyes begin to swell with tears. I've never known what it's like to not feel like an accident. To be loved unconditionally. I was just another bastard child that no one wanted. At least Phoenix got a chance to have something like that, even if it only lasted a few moments.

The ball of light flies past us, shooting off the cliff like a bullet. It lands in the water without creating a splash or ripple. Suddenly, the water begins to bubble, and the light shines brighter, changing the water into a sea green hue.

"I'm getting so tired of swimming," I say, crossing my arms in annoyance.

Phoenix places his arm across my shoulder and says, "That's too bad."

Without warning, he lifts me from the ground, into his arms, and jumps off the cliff. I squeal out of surprise, but inside, I'm laughing at his audaciousness. We both crash into the water, separating instantly. I open my eyes underwater and find him swimming in front of me. He grabs my hand and leads me back to the surface.

* * *

I reach the surface, gasping for air. The time of day has changed from day to night. We're not even in a lake anymore, but a pool. Phoenix looks at me, and I can see the fear in his eyes. We both get out of the pool and begin to walk toward a house. The house is your typical, beautiful suburban home.

I ask, "Is this your home?"

He replies, "It was once. Until it all got taken away."

I see black smoke coming out of the second-floor window on the other side of the house, and my heart sinks.

"Hey, your house is on fire!" I exclaim in shock.

I follow the smoke with Phoenix slowly behind, and then I get to it. I see a teenage version of Phoenix climbing down the window, wearing only a robe. His mother is at the main end, holding the rope, guiding him down.

Teenage Phoenix makes it to the ground and yells, "Mom, forget the rope; I'm down. Now just jump, and I'll catch you!"

"No, you will hurt yourself or me. I'll be down, sweetie. I'm tying the rope. Just stay strong!" his mother yells before walking away from view.

He yells, "Mom, no!"

Teenage Phoenix is panicking. His mom yells his name once more before a burst of flames escapes the window where she was just standing.

"Mom! Oh, shit! Mom, say something please!" he cries in horror.

The police and fire sirens can be heard in the background. Soon, a crew of firemen run toward Phoenix and grab him, taking him to safety. He begins fighting them off, yelling, "No, you can't take me away; my mom is still up there! She's still up there!"

Firefighters try to calm him down, reassuring him that they are going inside to rescue her or try the best they can. He gets taken away, looking back at his once beautiful home, now engulfed in flames.

"Oh, Phoenix."

That was all I could say to him. Everything he loved was ripped away from him overnight. I can't imagine the trauma he went through. I can't imagine living with those memories every day. I have my own unfortunate circumstances, but in no way, could I attempt to compare our pain.

"My dad and I lost everything. Everything. We got the official report two weeks after her funeral because they wanted to make sure there was a thorough investigation. It turned out the cause was an electrical problem. Nothing anyone could have caught, and no one to blame but fucking life." Tears fall onto his face, and he quickly dries them, breaking my heart.

Out of impulse, I hug him, squeezing my hold and wishing it could somehow take some of his pain away. He grabs a hold of me, and I can tell he's trying to hold back his tears. "It's okay to cry. You're still human. A dead human, but still human," I say, chuckling nervously, unsure if my words are consoling.

I release myself from Phoenix to check and make sure he's okay. Wiping his eyes, he says, "Okay, I'm good. I'm switching my man button back on now."

"Please. Everyone knows firefighters have the biggest balls. Except maybe astronauts, but they're out of this world anyway," I say.

He laughs at my corny joke attempt, which makes me laugh, and I realize that light can be found in any circumstance. The ball of light flies past us, then straight through the fence where they led teenage Phoenix away. The fence gate begins to glow, calling us to it. We both move forward, not looking back and not giving in.

14

We find ourselves on the side of a road—a highway to be exact. Traffic is flowing casually, and it is still nighttime. As I begin to turn around, a car loses control, causing it to flip multiple times until it lands off the road turned upside-down.

"Shit!" I yell in shock.

Phoenix's Camaro comes speeding onto the scene merely seconds later. A twenty something version of Phoenix races out of the car to help the victims. He arrives at the wreck like superman, breaks the passenger's side window, and pulls a woman out of the car. She appears to have suffered sufficient damage; her face his bloody and bruised, along with her right leg, which means it's more than likely broken. She's crying her eyes out, but she's alive.

Past Phoenix carefully drags her away from the car, reassuring her that everything is going to be okay. The ambulance and police arrive at the scene, and they begin to take over from there. I watch the former

Phoenix in amazement. He's quietly standing on the side, and I notice that his hands are trembling. He begins rubbing them together in attempt to conceal his anxiousness.

A police officer walks up to Phoenix and asks him if he could be a witness and explain what caused the accident. He obliges with ease and begins his explanation of what he witnessed, as anyone else would in an instance like this.

"Wow, that was amazing! You're a real hero. Most people would have been afraid, but you knew what to do and you acted. Were you a firefighter here?" I ask.

"No. I was actually on my way home from college here. That lady was speeding and driving a bit erratically, and when she swerved into the far-right lane, she lost control, and the car flipped. I was only a few cars behind her and saw the whole thing. Luckily, no one was killed that day," he answers.

"Because of you," I say with confidence. Phoenix blushes and gives a coy grin.

He says, "I guess this was a turning point for me. It felt good to save that woman. As it was all happening, for some reason, I could hear my mom's voice again. I could hear her telling me not to be afraid. I wasn't going to let anyone else die in front of me. One of the cops was impressed, and recommended I consider being a firefighter or a police officer. I went straight home and did as much research as I possibly could on firefighting, and it all just clicked for me. I had finally found a way to take my pain and turn it into something positive and, in a way, pay homage to my mom. This moment was my big epiphany."

The ball of light appears over our heads, spinning around us. It starts circling downward, surrounding us until we are engulfed with light.

* * *

The light finally disappears, leaving us in an office room that has a perfect view of the city. I look around the office, and the only thing I notice is how there is nothing to notice. Everything is neatly clean and placed perfectly, but there isn't a single painting on the wall— only certificates regarding work regulations and personal academic achievements.

The ghost of Phoenix's past enters the room, along with his aging father. His father takes a seat behind his desk, looking up at his son. He queries, "So what's this meeting all about, son?"

"Well, Dad, you know I'm going to be graduating soon, and I've been throwing around ideas about what

I'm going to do next. I think I may finally have the answer," he confesses.

"Son, I thought we already agreed on law school then a career in politics. You will have money and power in the palm of your hands. What are you confused about?" his dad inquires.

"Maybe I don't care about having money or power. Maybe I want to serve society in a different way," Phoenix says in defense.

"Enlighten me, then. Tell me how you are going to serve society and maintain your current lifestyle. How will you take care of yourself when I'm not around anymore?" his dad asks in an exasperated tone.

"If I do this, all I ask for is your emotional support. I can take care of myself financially. I won't be able to live the same lifestyle; in fact, there will be a major life change, but I'm okay with it. The job I'll be doing will give me purpose for others, and not just for our family name. This job is bigger and more meaningful," past Phoenix replies.

"What is the job?" his father asks seriously.

Phoenix scratches the back of his head nervously, anticipating his father's reaction when he reveals his answer. "Firefighting," Phoenix answers concisely.

His dad bursts into laughter, slapping his desk and kicking his head back as he does it. If looks could kill, past Phoenix would have given his dad a heart attack at that very moment. It is never okay to laugh at your child's dream. I wouldn't laugh at anyone's dream, let alone my offspring. Even if I believed they had no chance, I would never ridicule them for wanting to achieve something.

"You know what, Dad, you can laugh all you want, but I already took the agility test and passed," Phoenix reveals.

His father silences himself. His mood has completely changed from hot to cold.

"Yeah, they told me I had the best time in twenty-five years. They are practically begging me to join, Dad. I got more praise from them that day than you have given me my entire life! Mom died, and you just sent me away to boarding school while you drowned yourself with your work, alcohol, and whores! I won't be anything like you. Unlike you, I'm going to make Mom proud." Phoenix speaks in full conviction.

"You listen to me, boy. Don't ever talk about your mom to me! Ever! You don't know what I went through to survive losing her and everything we built together! You're all I have left of her, son. I did my best with you! Maybe it wasn't good enough, but I tried even though every time I look in your goddamn eyes, I see her face. But that's not your fault! I did not pay tens of thousands of dollars for your education so you could be a firefighter. You think you're a man, but you don't know what those men have to go through. You will come back home begging me to take you back in because you aren't built for that life, son. I didn't raise you to be a member of that lifestyle. I raised you to become a public figure like me. You may have all this built-up resentment, and that's my fault, but don't throw your hard work away to spite me, son, because only you will lose. Everyone that plays with fire gets burned, and that's a fact." His dad speaks with frustration.

"I'm not trying to spite you, Dad. All of my life, I have done exactly what you wanted me to do, even though it was never good enough. Now for the first time, I am choosing something that I want to do. I don't need to be a superhero to save someone's life. Don't forget; I do know what it's like to be in a burning building. I have lived that life, and it is because of it that I feel like I should do this," Phoenix justifies.

"Son, what happened to your mom was not your fault. It never was. I never blamed you for it, if that's what you think. I sent you away because I couldn't be the dad you needed me to be. I'm trying to provide you a good life, but if you choose this, you can kiss my support goodbye. I refuse to watch my only son risk his life to become some grimy working man who can barely pay his bills. Worst case scenario is you die playing hero, and my legacy will be gone forever."

"I don't need you to pay my way. All I needed was your support, but if you're going to be a selfish asshole, I'll be on my way. Firefighters look after each other, which is more than I can ask for from you," past Phoenix says as he turns around to leave his father's office.

"I'll be seeing you again. We will see who is right," his dad says.

"Yes, you will see me, Dad. You will be watching me save lives. Can't get righter than that." Phoenix walks out of the room, lighting up the doorway.

"Parents always act like they know everything when they are just as clueless as us," I say to him.

Phoenix shrugs his shoulders and says, "I guess all parents have their ideal child in their minds. I know I always hated that about my dad. He was always pushing me to do and act the way he wanted me to, but never took the time to ask what I liked. I'm not a sculpture; you can't just mold me into whatever shape you want and expect me to stand there and take it. I'm a person, not property. To be fair, I wasn't raised under ordinary circumstances, though," Phoenix says.

"At least you found a home at the firehouse, right?" I ask, trying to turn his frown upside down.

He smiles, nodding in agreement. "Yes, I did. There were six men stationed with me, and they took me under their wings. They showed me what it means to be a brother and to look after one another. The firehouse was my sanctuary; I could finally be the man I always wanted to be. I am proud to have worked alongside such brave men. Honorable men. I have a lot of regrets, but becoming a firefighter is not one. I loved my job, and I always felt valued. I never got that anywhere else. My dad was right about one thing, though; no one plays with fire and doesn't get burned."

"I guess we should move on now, huh?" I suggest.

He nods, and we walk toward the shining doorway, knowing that with each door we cross, we get closer to either absolution or execution. Anywhere but the latter.

15

I take my first step through to the other side, feeling concrete scraping the bottom of my feet. As soon as I'm across, I'm greeted with smoke from a burning building in front of me, causing me to cover my face to block the element. I find Phoenix leaning on the side of an ambulance truck parked across the street.

I walk over to him, and I notice a melancholy expression on his face. "Hey, what's wrong? Is this one of the bad days?"

"No, it's actually one of the good days. This was my first serious fire call as a rookie. I started as a search and rescuer, which isn't typical protocol, so I had a lot to prove. Once you have proven you can do the job, then you are free to fulfill your purpose: to save people. When you have such a daring goal like that, and the day comes when you can't do it anymore, it's devastating," Phoenix says.

A firefighter runs out of the burning building holding a woman in his arms. He's running toward the ambulance. A paramedic opens the door from the inside and pulls out the stretcher. I step a little closer to observe the scene.

The fireman lays the woman on the stretcher, and the paramedics immediately place an oxygen mask on her. The woman appears weak, but begins to gain some strength as her breathing regulates. The fireman takes off his head gear, revealing a sweaty but enthusiastic Phoenix.

Another fireman walks up to him and says, "Slow down, rook; the rest of us need a job too."

Another fireman welcomes himself into the conversation by stating, "You wouldn't believe how this fire started. Someone has been burning pinewood in their fireplace. Yes, pinewood! Sounds like an arsonist to me. I refuse to believe someone could be so asinine. Is the girl going to be okay?"

Former Phoenix answers, "Yes, she's going to be fine. Is everyone accounted for, sir?"

"Yes. This was a lucky call. The foundation is completely ruined, but there were no casualties. Even the pets made it out; I think I saw Jason rescue a hamster. Anyways, good job; you saved lives today. Now get your ass back to the station; you earned a break."

"Yes, sir. Thank you," past Phoenix says.

The paramedic closes the door and drives off moments later. A film crew arrives and immediately begins to inquire about details.

"Not today, shitheads," says the chief as he's walking off.

"Sir, is it okay if we film your men doing their work? We just want a good story!" the reporter shouts to him.

He replies, "The only thing you can film is my tired ass walking away!"

The film crew turns their attention away to the other firemen in attempt to get a story out of them. I turn to Phoenix, who is smiling at the man walking away.

"Was that your boss?" I ask.

"Yes, he was the chief. One of the best," Phoenix replies.

As I'm about to reply, I notice the light-made doorway that's been our main source of transportation. "Our ride is here," I say as I begin walking toward our next destination. I can hear Phoenix following behind as I cross through the doorway.

* * *

Once I cross through, I am met with a large, black cloud of smoke along with flames dancing right above the ceilings. I jump back from shock, and when I do, I feel Phoenix's body right behind me. A section of the ceiling collapses right behind us, causing me to panic and scream. Phoenix grabs my shoulders and says, "It's okay, Cadence; we can't get hurt in here. I remember this place."

We hear a loud crash coming from the front of the building. We walk to the hallway where the noise traveled down. I see a broken-down door and three firemen searching and rescuing.

The fire begins gaining momentum, with its roaring flames lighting up shades of blue, red, and amber each time it licks its next possession to destroy. The firefighters find a woman lying unconscious, so two of them go on each side and lift her up. They place her in the third fireman's arms, bridal style, and he carries her from harm's way.

The other two firemen begin searching for more people to rescue. With their gas masks, it's impossible to tell who is who, but since we haven't left yet, old Phoenix must be one of those men.

One fireman walks down the hallway and stops at a door. He opens it and yells for his partner. His partner comes along, and they both run inside the room.

Moments later, one fireman runs out carrying two small children covered in a blanket. His partner is soon behind, carrying what appears to be three children. It's as smoky as an inferno inside, but I can see three pairs of tiny feet being carried away to safety.

They run out of the building in record time, considering the heavy weight they must be carrying. The roof begins to collapse around us, causing the flames to rise higher and more fiercely from the fresh oxygen coming through. As the last fireman runs out of the building, the doorway lights up, signaling our ride.

"Come on!" Phoenix yells, grabbing my hand and guiding me out of this building and on to somewhere else.

I was not prepared for all that intensity. It was amazing to witness such an act of heroism between all three men. This may have been just another day for him, but not to me. I've seen a handful of house fires passing through places, but I have never personally been in one. Luckily, being dead, we can't feel the heat anyway.

Through the passageway we go, leaving that destructive fire behind. My eyes are closed, and my hand is still squeezing Phoenix's when we cross over to the other side.

* * *

I hear a crowd applause, and I open my eyes to look at my surroundings. We are standing in the middle of an aisle at a ceremony. There isn't an empty seat in the house. Everyone is dressed in formal attire, and I notice a lot of firemen sitting in the front section wearing their Class A uniforms.

I look at the stage and see a man at the podium. He bends his head slightly at the microphone before saying, "Thank you."

Just then, I recognize that the man speaking is Phoenix's father. I turn to Phoenix, and his eyes are glued to his dad's. I turn my attention to him as well.

His father speaks again. "I couldn't be prouder to name this next fireman. Fireman Phoenix Armstrong, my son, has only been active for eighteen months, and he has already accomplished the highest honor a firefighter can receive. I thought he had lost his mind when he first told me the news. In fact, that's exactly what I told him. All parents develop certain aspirations for their children—me included. I held onto those aspirations so tightly that for a while, I couldn't accept his decision, and as a result, we didn't speak for a long time. Now I hold this gold medal of valor with my son's name etched on it, and I feel like the biggest fool in the world. Every father's dream is to be a hero to his son, but for me, my son is my hero. You inspire me to be a better man, and I know your mother would be so proud. She always saw the world in you, son, and I'm so proud of the man you've become. Today, I award this medal of valor to Fireman Phoenix Armstrong serving Firehouse 26."

Former Phoenix, who is sitting on the side of the stage, rises from his chair to accept his award and gives his father a big hug. Phoenix stands next to the two men that were with him that day, and they all salute the audience, wearing matching medals. The audience begins to clap.

"Before we wrap this up, we have surprise guests for the men of honor." His father walks toward the back curtain and partially lifts it.

A few moments later, the five children and the teacher that were rescued come running out, startling everyone. The children all attack the firemen with hugs and gratitude, with the teacher following, shaking their hands and thanking them for their service. The entire room begins laughing and clapping at this moment. The firemen all seem moved by this gesture. Phoenix looks really gratified. He has a smile that only death could remove. He looks fulfilled. His father has the same look on his face. It's such a beautiful moment for everyone.

I look over to my Phoenix, and he's crying in silence. I place my hand on his shoulder out of concern.

Before I can speak, the ball of light flies down the aisle, zooming past us at the speed of sound. It flies through the exit, lighting the doorway simultaneously.

"You go ahead. I'm going to take a minute to myself. This is the last time I'll ever be here, so I wanna savor what I can until it all ends."

It all ends. Hearing those words, for some reason, feels like a stab to the heart. I don't believe he's giving up already. Maybe my paranoia has finally got the best of me, and I'm overreacting.

Still, I can't bring myself to ask him about it, so instead, I just say, "Okay."

I walk through the doorway, crossing into the unknown, scared but motivated to win this spiritual conquest. I know that when my time comes, I will be terrified and vastly unprepared, but I feel that I still have enough self-preservation to combat all of those disadvantages. It's too bad that instinct didn't kick in before I decided to kill myself. I guess you die and you learn.

* * *

I notice that I'm inside Phoenix's firehouse, complete with sliding poles leading up to the top floor and a few fire trucks and supplies filling the room. I hear a hose turn on, instantly grabbing my attention, and I follow the sound. I walk up to a fire truck nearby and find past Phoenix holding a water hose in one hand and a sponge in the other. I can hear him humming a song, but his mood appears to be stoic.

"I always hated washing the truck, which is why I always got assigned to do it. He told me doing what you hate builds character. What bullshit," my Phoenix says, causing me to jump.

I turn around to greet him with an embarrassed smile, and he returns a playful smile back. "I'm glad you're here," I say.

A fire truck drives into the station, parking in its designated spot. Three firemen come out of the vehicle and take off their hats. One fireman walks over to Phoenix and asks to speak to him. Phoenix agrees, sets his equipment down, and gives the man his full attention.

I can't exactly make out what they are saying, but Phoenix's body language is enough indication to know that they're not offering a promotion. As the fireman tells him the information, Phoenix's face changes from stoic to despair, then anger, then despair again. He shakes the fireman's hand and walks off into the back. He forcefully pushes open the exit door, causing it to slam against the wall.

"My dad was killed in a car accident. That was what he told me. He wasn't perfect at all, but we had just patched things up in our relationship, and then he was gone. I can't really explain what losing both parents feels like, except that it changes you. I rescued losers every day that destroyed themselves and their communities by cooking drugs, drinking and driving, and any other awful thing a person could do. My dad was honorable and loved serving his city, and yet he dies at the age of 54. He deserved so much more."

"He did, and so did you," I say, fighting back my tears for his heartbreaking circumstances. His life was like mine in a sense; whenever you manage to take one step forward, you get blown back three.

"I think I know what may be coming next, and I'm not ready for it. I thought that living this all before would make it easier to watch, but it's worse. I could be fearless when it came to emergencies and fighting fires, but this—facing myself—is the hardest thing I've ever had to do," Phoenix says.

"You won't be alone," I reply somberly. I know that the closer we get to his demise, the sooner I will be all alone again, just like before. If he finds peace, nirvana, heaven, or whatever amazing place that takes us away from here, then at least I will know for sure that I have a shot.

I can't help but feel the hole getting deeper and deeper in my heart as we pass through each door. Saying goodbye to the one person that saved me from all this is too much to imagine right now. A teardrop slips from my left eye, sliding down my face. I wipe it away and pull myself together. I promised myself that I would help him see this through and find peace. It's weird how crying is the only human thing left we can do, but I know now isn't the time to break down.

"Are you okay?" Phoenix asks.

"I'll make it," I reply honestly.

"Look!" Phoenix shouts, pointing toward the exit.

The doorway exit is lit up like the sun, with all its power and light radiating from within. Phoenix takes a deep breath and says, "It's now or never."

We walk through the door reluctantly, knowing that each countless door will bring us closer to our final destination.

* * *

We step into a living room, and I see past Phoenix sitting on a couch with a young woman. He's in a black tank top with gray pajamas, and he's developed a five o'clock shadow, which is throwing me off because I've only seen him clean-shaven up until now. The woman has on a casual, pink, floral dress and gold sandals.

She's very attractive, with long, brunette hair, big, blue eyes, and a small frame.

I'm assuming that they were dating because they're both holding beer bottles and watching television.

I can tell that this is Phoenix's old place because of the video game posters and barely clothed models taped on the walls. This room screams man cave. His home is just big enough to fit all of his furniture and still have a decent walking space, but he's definitely downsized from his father's mansion, I'm sure. There are brick walls with a wooden floor and a door that leads to a small patio. It's a very cozy house for a young, single man, I must admit.

Phoenix says to me, "Oh man, I miss this place. I got twenty-five percent off rent every month for being a firefighter, which was great. Firefighters don't get paid what they deserve, but at least there are perks from time to time. I had some great times in this house. Though this is not one of them, I'm afraid."

"Did you have a fight with your girlfriend?" I ask curiously.

"Yes, but it's complicated. I was a hero, but that doesn't mean I was a perfect one," he answers.

The woman gets up from the couch angrily, towering over past Phoenix. Looking up at her in confusion, he says, "What is your problem, Elizabeth? What did I do now?"

Elizabeth replies, "My problem is that it's been two months, and all we've done is hang around your place doing only what you want to do. You used to take me out, but ever since your dad died, you hardly pay me any attention! Don't you love me? Don't you want us to build something?"

Past Phoenix takes another swig of his beer before saying, "I don't know what you want me to say. I told you from the beginning, I don't want to commit. I'm never going to be a family guy, so stop trying to change my mind. You're a great girl, Elizabeth, and having you here is great. But you have no idea the kind of baggage that comes with being a firefighter."

She replies, "I want to be the one to help carry your baggage, but you don't want me. I know being a fireman's wife is a hard life, but I love you. Having a family is the only true way to carry on your legacy. People always forget you long after you're gone. I know what happened to your mom was tragic—"

Phoenix quickly gets up from the couch and interjects, "Don't talk about my mom."

"You have to talk to someone!" Elizabeth yells in frustration.

"I'm not talking about my mother," former Phoenix reiterates.

"I know losing your mom was tragic and you don't want to risk that happening again, but let me reassure you that it won't. You won't lose me. We got something special, Phoenix, and I want us to grow together," Elizabeth confesses.

"You got me all figured out, huh? You think I'm just some lost little boy who needs to be taken care of, but I'm not. I'm a damn hero. I risk my life every day to save people. I don't need a family to validate my existence. I'm sorry, Elizabeth; I can't give you what you want," past Phoenix says.

Elizabeth sets her beer bottle on the coffee table and grabs her purse from the couch. She looks at Phoenix and says, "I'm done. I can't be with you anymore if we're not going anywhere. I think I deserve better than that."

"Okay. Well, I'm sorry you feel that way. I wish you the best," past Phoenix says.

"That's all you have to say to me? 'I wish you the best,'" she says bitterly.

Past Phoenix crosses his arms and says, "I'm not sure how you want me to respond. You're the one wanting to walk away, and I'm letting you."

Elizabeth screeches, grabs the beer bottle from the table, and throws it at his head. Former Phoenix ducks just in time, causing the bottle to hit the front door and shatter. He stands up with a look of shock and confusion.

"I hate you! You may be a hero, but you're a heartless son of a bitch! That's why you're going to end up all alone!" Elizabeth yells, walking out the door.

"You leave my fucking mom out of this! I'd rather be alone than spend another second with you! Fuck!" Phoenix retorts furiously.

Elizabeth exits through the doorway, causing it to light up. Past Phoenix walks off toward the patio, I'm guessing to cool down from their argument. I look at my Phoenix, and he seems upset by this memory. He turns away, avoiding eye contact with me.

"I know you probably think I'm a jerk. I didn't mean to be a prick, but I didn't know how to open up to anyone. Firefighters can't talk to normal people about their job; they can't fathom it. She was a great person, though, and I should've treated her better. I should've treated all of my exes better than I did. I was still dealing with my father's death as well. I had to deal with the fact that the only family I had left was my fire family. Promise me you won't think less of me. I don't want you to think less of me," Phoenix says.

"Of course, I don't think less of you. I could never. There is nothing wrong with not wanting a family. Maybe you could have handled it better, but that doesn't mean you shouldn't be forgiven. You're still the same hero to me. Besides, you haven't seen the shit I've done. I'd be a hypocrite if I were to judge you because of one bad moment," I say.

Phoenix turns around and looks at me. He says, "Thanks, Cadence. You've really become a great friend, which is something I never thought I'd find in this place."

"So, have you," I say, touched by his words.

He grabs my hand, lacing his fingers into mine, and says, "Let's get out of here."

"Ride or die," I say, looking into his eyes as he looks into mine.

We step through the door, welcomed by fire once again.

* * *

We're standing in the corner of a dismantled living room bathed in flames and black smoke. Suddenly, the wooden floor rises from under us, splitting in half and releasing the flames hiding underneath.

"The fucking floor is collapsing!" I yell, gripping what's left of the floor.

Phoenix follows suit, getting low as well. He replies, "That's because it's a basement fire. They're dangerous and unpredictable!"

Another part of the floor collapses, causing the room to shake. I'm holding onto the floor as tightly as I can in all this fiery chaos. The last thing I need is to end up at the bottom of a basement inferno.

A fireman comes running inside from a hallway in front of us, heading toward the front door. Three firemen come running behind him, all trying to run on a shaky, unstable floor. As they get closer to the door, the ceiling caves in on top of the group, sparing one of them. The fireman at the door turns around to help. He grabs his ax and uses it to lift the burning rubble off his injured crew.

The floor collapses from under the fallen men's feet. The two firemen both jump toward them, failing to save them from the fall.

"We have to go now!" one of the firemen yells.

That's when I realize that the guy yelling is Phoenix. He picks himself up and helps his partner stand. The roof suddenly caves in on top of them, causing Phoenix to fall into the hole, suffering a similar fate to his teammates.

The other fireman is pinned to the floor, but still alive. He reaches for the radio attached to his shoulder and yells, "MAYDAY! First floor! Mayday! Mayday! Chief, I'm stuck, and the rest of the team is gone. The whole infrastructure is falling around me. We should have never been in here! MAYDAY!"

The fireman starts coughing and wheezing. I see him struggle to reach into his pocket to retrieve a miniature bottle of alcohol. He twists the top off with one hand and downs it all before choking on the thick, black smoke surrounding him.

I look over to the real Phoenix, and he seems as if the wind has been knocked out of him. I say to him, "He was right; this house is too unstable. There was nothing you could have done."

A chunk of burning rubble falls onto the floor, causing me to scream. The front doorway lights up, giving me newfound hope inside.

"It's about time! Thank you!" I yell in relief.

Phoenix lifts me up from the ground, and we make our way to the exit. As we're leaving, ghosts of firemen run into the building, including the nozzle man, who quickly begins putting out the fire. Two other ghostly firemen lift the debris off the injured firemen and carry him out. Another group of firemen run inside with a ladder and rope, ready to search and rescue.

I stand at the exit, pointed toward my freedom, only to turn away to witness the ghosts of his past. Phoenix probably doesn't even remember this part; at least I hope not. The best thing for anybody at that point is just to stay knocked out.

"Wow," Phoenix says, eyes transfixed on the scene before him.

We take a final look before crossing over into the next part of Phoenix's story.

16

We step into a dimly lit, single hospital room with a pretty banged up Phoenix in it. He's lying slightly upright on the bed because of the brace on his neck. He's got burn bandages all over his left arm and large cast on his right leg. His face has only a few scratches, which is a miracle to me, but his bottom lip is busted and slightly bleeding.

A man walks into the room, removes his jacket, and hangs it on the coat rack.

The injured Phoenix speaks. "Chief? Chief, is that you?"

"Hey, son. It's me. You sound a lot better. How do you feel?" The chief sits next to the bed and takes out a set of rosary beads from his pocket.

"Is it bad, chief?" former Phoenix asks, clenching his free hand into a fist with all his might.

"You need to rest and heal; that's the only thing that matters now," the chief replies.

"Am I finished? Will I ever fight fires again? Cause that's the only thing that matters to me," Phoenix asks.

"You know, Phoenix, you should be grateful you're still breathing. Two of your own died that day, and I had to be the one to deliver the news to their wives," the chief replies.

"I don't have a wife or any family left. All I have is firefighting. I know you think you're sparing my feelings, but it's killing me inside not knowing for sure. Tell me, please," Phoenix cries.

"I'm sorry, Phoenix; the damage was just too great," the chief begins.

Phoenix lets out a cry before covering his mouth with his free hand, muffling the noise.

The chief grabs his arm in consolation and continues. "They are going to do their best to try to get you standing again. It's going to be a long, difficult recovery, but I want you to know that I'm not going anywhere. You know your brothers will always be here. You are not alone. You're a hero, and you did your job, son. You're one of the finest firemen I've ever known. I'm privileged to have had you on my team, son."

"What am I going to do?" Phoenix cries, tears pouring from his face as if gray clouds were raining above him.

"We get through this, son. We get through it. You need to focus on healing and getting through physical therapy. Take it one day at a time. Your life will come together again. Always remember that you're a hero," the chief answers.

A nurse walks into the room, maneuvering a medical supply cart. She closes the blinds and adjusts the light in the room, making it brighter. "Hello. I'm so sorry to cut this short, but visiting hours have ended. Feel free to come back in the morning."

"Okay, thank you," the chief says, standing up. He looks at Phoenix and says, "We're all here for you. Get some rest, son. We'll see you soon. Tomorrow we are going to bring all the gifts and cards from people; you will really like it. Don't let this bring you down, Phoenix."

The chief exits the room, and the doorway lights up. I turn to my Phoenix, who has his attention on the nurse preparing to change his piss bag. I say, "Hey, we don't have to watch all this; the doorway is giving us an out."

I notice his hands beginning to twitch, so he rubs them together to combat it. He begins shaking his head like he doesn't want to leave. "This is it. If I leave here, Cadence, the next memory is more than likely me killing myself, like the rest. I don't know what's going to happen to me. Facing my fate terrifies me. I've never been so scared, and I have no control over any of this. I'm afraid to move," Phoenix says, panicking.

His words hit me like a train, and I feel like a glass statue that's been shattered into pieces. This is almost the end of the road. I can feel that incessant urge in my brain to panic and invent all types of crazy scenarios that could possibly happen, but instead, I focus on Phoenix. I've been keeping myself together pretty well, considering all the experiences we've been through. Also, I've been seeing the outside perspective the whole time. Phoenix's path seems to be ending, and whatever happens after that, it's my turn. I'm next in line.

I place my hand on his shoulder, and he places his hand over mine in return. I say, "We have to keep moving; it's the only way. I got you."

He nods his head, concurring, and releases my hand. We both walk through the doorway, understanding that there is no escaping the inevitable.

* * *

We step into Phoenix's bedroom. His past self is lying upright on his bed, with his fireman uniform laid neatly next to him. He tightens the suspenders on his pants before lifting his left leg up to place it inside. He rolls over to his left side and picks up his right leg, using his right arm to adjust himself until his pants are on properly. He lifts his body to sit up straight, causing him stress and discomfort. He buckles the suspenders over his navy shirt and puts on his boots that were lying near him. He then puts on his jacket and reaches under his pillow. He pulls out a small black box and opens it, revealing the medal he was honored with. He removes it and puts it on, hiding it under his shirt.

He grabs his wheelchair that was strategically placed next to the bed, gripping the armrests to scoot himself over, grunting and moaning until he finally reaches his wheelchair. He catches his breath, taking in slow and deep breaths, having just applied all that pressure onto his upper body. Once he's gathered his strength, he wipes the sweat off his brow and rolls out of the bedroom, lighting the doorway behind him.

I stand there spellbound at his condition. I never thought his damage had gotten that bad. I look at the real Phoenix, and his expression shows solemnity.

"I had gone through two spinal surgeries and six months of physical therapy just to lose my legs anyway. I just didn't see a future anymore. I couldn't be a fireman; I could barely be a man," Phoenix says.

"That's not true," I inject curtly.

"Yes, it is, Cadence. I never walked again until I died and came here, which is the only good thing this place has given me. Without my legs, I became useless to everyone when I was alive. I couldn't! I couldn't! I couldn't be the man I once was. Why didn't I just die in that fire with the rest of my crew? I would have at least been remembered as a hero," Phoenix weeps.

"You will always be remembered as a hero! You helped so many people, and you never asked for anything in return. I get it; I do. You were a superhero, and being a firefighter was your superpower. When you couldn't do it anymore, you got lost," I say.

"Something like that," Phoenix says, chuckling at himself while wiping tears away.

"I think we have more in common than we realize. You know, being a firefighter wasn't the only thing you had to offer. You possessed a lot of skills. Maybe you could have found a way to live with it, but I'm not going to pretend like I understand what you were going through."

Phoenix nods his head and says, "I guess I did rob myself of the chance to find out if I could be happy. I was so caught up in what I didn't have, I took for granted that I still had my life. Even if it wasn't the one I expected, in hindsight, I must say that I should have stuck it out. I see that now."

"Are you ready?" I inquire, staring into his aching baby blues.

"No," he says, laughing. I join him, despite the pain I'm feeling.

This is it. This is the end for you, my friend—my only friend left at all. Fresh, warm tears begin staining my face, and I quickly cover my vulnerable brown eyes.

"Are you okay, Cadence?" Phoenix asks, worriedly.

"Yes. I'm just scared too, that's all. I'm holding it in as best I can," I admit.

"Well, no sense in stalling any longer. We've come this far now," he says.

He takes my hand, and I feel my feet being led toward the doorway. We stop right in front, and he looks at me and says, "I'm so glad it was you I got to be here with. I wouldn't have made it with anyone else."

"Likewise," I reply, giving him the warmest smile I could muster. He returns a satisfied smirk, and we cross through the doorway hand in hand, ready for what's to come.

* * *

We cross to the other side and find ourselves back in Phoenix's garage, like he had predicted. His mother's car is sitting in the center of the room, but unlike before, it's glowing. There is bright, white light gleaming through the windows of the car, ejecting a magnetic feeling of belonging.

Phoenix lets go of my hand and walks over to his former possession, captivated by the light as well. "What do you think this means?" Phoenix asks, examining the car nervously.

I look over to the exit, and I see that the doorway is still glowing. I guess it's officially time for us to part. That's life; you can always count on goodbyes. I look at Phoenix and take him all in. I try to remember every detail of him as I can, and I hold back the tears that are so furiously ready to be released.

"It means it's time for you to move on. You made it. This is your redemption, Phoenix. You're free," I say, holding back my flooding tears.

Phoenix replies, "What about you? Us? We're moving on together; I have to help you see your life through."

"No, no, no," I say. "We have our own path; you completed yours, and you get to move on. It's right here waiting for you. For once in your life, you get to save yourself. So save yourself."

"No, you're not getting rid of me that easy. It's only fair that I see your life since you saw mine," he replies.

"Now isn't the time for jokes," I say sternly. "This is a good thing. This means I have hope to find peace. In a way, you've given me a guide, and I thank you, and I'll always be with you in some way. Phoenix, you have shown me what it means to do something good—to be good. I'm carrying you with all the other people I've ever loved, and I'll find my way. I promise you. Maybe we can both meet on the other side. Together."

I walk up to Phoenix and hug him. He hesitates before placing his arms around me, hugging me tightly. My ear is resting on his chest, and in this moment, I hear his faint heartbeat. It's barely audible, but it's present, and it sounds like a metronome. The imaginary dam that was holding back my tears finally breaks, and my eyes begin flooding. I release myself from him before I soak his shirt.

I wipe my eyes, look at him one final time, and say, "This is so hard. I'm so happy for you, Phoenix. You deserve to be happy."

"You too, Cadence. I promise we won't be apart for long. I will find a way to get to you because that's what we do for the ones we love," he says, giving me that same boyish grin that I've grown to care for.

I stare deep into his blue eyes one last time, and right before I get completely lost in them, I look away.

"Goodbye," I say, walking backward toward the doorway.

Phoenix opens the driver side door and replies, "Goodbye."

I watch him get inside and disappear into the light—gone forever.

I gasp, trying to calm the mixed feeling inside of me. I feel a deepening hole in my chest being fueled by the deafening silence. It's my turn to face my darkness. My life is now being thrown in front of me, and I only have myself to lean on.

Maybe it's for the best that I'm alone. I've had some pretty disturbing things happen that were always hard to talk about. I can be strong, though. I have to be strong. I can't buckle under pressure when my soul is at stake. I can feel my feet finally land on the other side, and I step into it with my head high and my spirit still strong.

17

I open my eyes once I'm across the other side, and I see a confused Phoenix staring back at me. I hold my hand out in defense, and take slow, careful steps toward him.

"Is that really you, Phoenix?" I ask, desperately wanting it to be him.

"Yeah, I'm back. Totally called it," Phoenix gloats.

I run into his arms, gripping his body with all my emotional being. He hugs me back, and I begin giggling, which makes him giggle in return. I can't believe he's staying here with me. I always had to work hard for everything I gained because in my life, there were no miracles. For once, I got a miracle.

"I'm so happy you're here. I know we can get through all my baggage together, and maybe then we can finally be free," I say releasing him.

"Let's not wait any longer," Phoenix says. He looks away, observing our surroundings.

I look around to assess our situation, and though I feel an odd familiarity, I don't recognize this place. We're in a hospital room with two hospital beds, both covered by privacy curtains. I look toward the exit door, and I see my grandmother walking into the room. She walks straight to the first bed and opens the curtain, revealing my mother holding the newborn version of me.

"That's my mom and my grandma, and that's me when I was a baby," I say in awe.

I take in my maternal relatives with their mocha-colored skin and straight, black hair. My mother looks exhausted, which, of course, is because she had just given birth to me, but I almost forgot how beautiful she was. My grandmother looks lovely as well, wearing her dashiki dress with her long, black hair styled in a single braid.

"Wow. Now I see where you get your beauty," Phoenix says, making me smile a mile wide.

My grandmother speaks. "Desiree, I finally got in touch with him. He said he couldn't get away, but he will be here tomorrow to see her and sign the paperwork."

My mother's expression grows into frustration, and she kisses me on my tiny forehead before reaching over and placing me in the hospital crib. She turns to my grandma and says, "I knew it. I knew he was going to pick his family over her. He can't even do right by his own damn child!"

My newborn self begins crying, and my mother quickly begins rocking the crib and humming. When the crying stops, my mother begins speaking again. "Look how precious she is. She's going to be so beautiful. Look at how pale she is; she's going to have a beautiful complexion. She's too beautiful to not be wanted."

My mother bursts to tears, and my grandmother consoles her. I watch the scene unfold never knowing all of this. I never knew he didn't show up the day I was born, and I never knew my mom was that happy about me. Judging by the situation, I always felt that I was more of an inconvenience to everyone. Seeing this now makes me sad, but the love and appreciation from my mother was a pleasant surprise.

I speak to Phoenix. "My father was never present in my life. Not because he was in jail, not because it was hard for a black man to get by, not even because he didn't love my mother. He was never there because he never wanted to be. I accepted this fact a long time ago. I always thought my mom resented me for it, but I see she really did love me, and it was the circumstances. We're all just victims of circumstance."

Phoenix puts his hand on my shoulder, and I can feel the sympathy within his touch. Softly, he says, "Cadence, the doorway is glowing. Are you ready to go?"

I nod profusely before uttering, "Yeah." I take one final look before closing the privacy curtain. We silently exit this place and enter the next.

* * *

We arrive at the next destination, and the first person I see is my grandmother. I can hear a catchy rock song blasting across the room, with an electric guitar solo that's spellbinding. My grandmother is sitting in her auburn-hued rocking chair with her knitting kit in her hands. Suddenly, I feel like I've been through a time machine because I remember this event. I realize that I'm really in this shit, and my time of reckoning has arrived. Here we go.

My grandmother looks as relaxed as I always remembered her to be. She's wearing one of her signature dashiki shirts; this one in particular is long and honey brown with a multicolored patchwork design of primary colors and a simple, white tank top to complete her cultural style.

Suddenly, a five-year-old version of me appears in the living room, jumping around, headbanging, and singing along to the song. I was a cute kid with long, kinky curls, a heart-shaped face, and light brown skin with a bright smile that captured the essence of my free spirit.

Phoenix holds a surprised expression on his face, hiding behind his smile. "So, you were a rocker girl growing up?" he asks curiously.

I reply, "No. I was a rocker girl my whole life. It's my bliss."

"I...was not expecting that from you. I mean that in a good way. I'm pleasantly surprised, I promise. I do recall you saying you were a singer, now that I think about it," Phoenix says.

"I know. I had to bare all of the opinions, believe me. Not everyone had the same reaction as you. I was born in a small town called West Memphis, and they believed that people who listened to rock music were devil worshipers and couldn't be saved. Being black only made it even more taboo, but I didn't care. I just wanted to be myself," I confess.

"Wow. Did you believe in God?" Phoenix asks, raising his left eyebrow, awaiting my answer.

"No, I didn't," I answer honestly.

He replies, "I lost my faith after my mother passed. My parents were both Catholic, but we only went to church every other month, and they weren't very strict. After my mom died, I wanted to believe more than ever, but I couldn't. Now that I'm here, I still don't know if there is a God. I haven't seen Him. Maybe we are experiencing this to become worthy of Him. I don't know. At least we know now that there's more after we die. Maybe if we had known that, things would have been different for us."

"Maybe," I say, absorbing his truth into my own until the parts I want to keep become a part of me. The truth is that even though this isn't the best destination, at least there are places you go next.

My mother enters the living room wearing her work scrubs, and cuts the radio off. My younger self stops dancing and covers her mouth, anticipating the scolding that is about to unfold. My grandmother, still rocking in her chair, looks up at my mother for a moment, then continues knitting a pair of socks.

My mother speaks. "Why do you let her listen to that mess? You know how weird that is for a little black girl to be," she points toward little me, "behaving like that? She needs to know that she's not white, and she will never be treated like she is."

My grandmother looks up and says, "She don't need to be ashamed of liking that music when that music is in our blood. We share blood with the father of blues. It's good to see some of our kin keeping his spirit alive."

My mother throws her hands in the air and says, "I can't talk to you," and walks out of the room. The little girl that was once me angrily runs out of the front door, lighting the doorway behind her.

I drag out a long sigh before forcing myself to put one foot in front of the other to get to the next moment in my life. I'm trying to remember all the good and bad things in my life to possibly deduce what could be coming next, but my efforts are futile. It's a pointless task anyway, like sitting in a rocking chair; I can sit and rock back and forth to keep me busy, but it won't get me anywhere. I guess I'll get off this metaphorical chair and put my energy towards whatever is coming next.

* * *

We cross through the door of light, and it takes us to my old elementary school. I'm standing right in front of it on this beautiful, clear, blue-skied day, watching children run out of the building. Some are running toward the buses, others running toward parents waiting out front to take them home, and other kids standing around in groups, chatting their heads off.

Out of the door comes myself—my eight-year-old self, to be exact—running with a trophy about half her size and a gold medal hanging around her neck. I elbow Phoenix to get his attention and point him toward the younger me.

Excitedly, the other me runs up toward my mother, who is standing on the sidewalk, waiting. She's wearing her scrubs from her sterile processing job. She worked multiple jobs, so seeing her at all was a big deal. We walk up a little closer to view the scene.

"What's all this?" my mother asks, happily surprised.

"Mom, I won the spelling bee! I beat every kid in the school, and they gave me this trophy, and I get to join the state spelling bee competition, and they say that's out of town!" younger me says jubilantly.

"That's wonderful! I had no idea you even signed up. What a day!" My mother hugs younger me in triumph, and that proud moment I felt back then comes crashing back into my heart. "I can't wait to tell everybody how smart and capable my daughter is!"

"Can you tell Dad? Maybe he'll want to see my trophy if you tell him how big it is, and we can have dinner or something." younger me pleads. I can feel Phoenix's eyes on me suddenly, but I continue to watch the scene anyway.

"Cadence, you know that's not possible. He won't show up; he never shows up. The sooner you accept that, the better things will be," my mother says sternly, breaking that little ounce of spirit, I had left back then.

I watch my little head hang low and my mouth quiver. My mother lifts my head up by my chin and says, "Hey, dry it up. I'm raising you to be strong, so you can handle what life throws at you. You don't have anything to feel sorry about. He's the problem, not you. You did good today; you should feel proud. I'm proud. As a matter of fact, let's celebrate. How about your favorite happy meal?" my mom asks cheerfully, trying to change my mood.

"Okay," younger me says in voice of discontent. My mother guides younger me along the sidewalk, walking into the distance, away from us forever.

I can still feel Phoenix's eyes on me, so I finally turn to him and say, "That was just me doing anything I could to get my father's attention. Frankly, anyone's attention. I never got the attention I wanted; not during my childhood, at least, but that's when it counts the most."

The ball of light appears, circling around us then flying inside the elementary building, lighting the doorway to our next place. A dark feeling sets upon me as we walk toward the door. Phoenix grabs my hand and passes me a reassuring grin. I retaliate, and we continue this walk down memory lane.

* * *

On the other side of the doorway, I find myself back in a familiar bedroom. This boyish bedroom decorated in every shade of blue didn't belong to me, nor did I ever wish to be in it. It took me years to break these memories, and here I am, suddenly back here again.

Phoenix takes a brief look around before asking, "Whose bedroom is this? Did you have a little brother?"

I avert my sad eyes before answering, "No. I was an only child. This room belonged to one of my mother's friend's sons. They used to babysit me when my mom had to work weekends." A single tear slips from my left eye, and I turn away, covering my eyes and wiping away the evidence.

"Where is this going?" Phoenix asks in a worried, slightly hoarse tone.

The boy I had been dreading to see walks into the bedroom. Looking at him now, he had to have been a preteen. He always carried himself like he was the big bully on the block, picking on anyone smaller than him—like me.

Eight-year-old me slowly walks into the room, leaving the door open. The boy slams the door, shouting, "What the hell I tell you? You always shut the door!"

"I'm sorry. I don't want to play house today. I don't like it. Please don't make me do it. I feel really sick," the little girl version of me pleads.

Emotions get the best of me, and I let a tear fall, even though I really got past it, despite nothing ever getting done about it. I look at Phoenix and notice that his jaw is anchored to the floor and both his hands are on his head, which is shaking slowly back and forth as if he can't believe his eyes.

The boy grabs younger me by the throat and spits, "I'll choke your ass if you don't get under the bed, and nobody ain't gonna do anything about it."

Crying, younger me wiggles her way out of the boy's hands and slowly crawls under the bed, with the boy following close behind.

Phoenix, carrying a distraught look on his face, asks, "How long did this go on? Did you ever tell anyone? Did that little monster get dealt with?"

"No, I never told anyone about it because I didn't think anyone would believe me. My mom was best friends with his mom, and she thought the world of him. He was a two-faced, maniacal bastard, and one day, we moved, and I didn't have to go there anymore, so I just kept it in. I learned to deal with it by developing my interest in rock music and books. Rock music saved me from the feeling of worthlessness I had my whole life. This sucked, but I overcame it and did my best to move forward."

"I'm sorry! I'm so sorry! I'm sorry!" Phoenix says in a regretful, hurt tone.

Phoenix pulls me into a hug, and I gratefully return it. A strong male figure to look up to was never present in my life, and I spent my adult life constantly searching for it. Here is the ultimate male figure holding me, touching my fears and telling them to fuck off. It's a foreign feeling, having a man care so much without having a sexual agenda. I imagine that this is what having a father feels like, not that I'll ever know.

The doorway lights up, and we release each other from our hug. "Let's get the hell out of here," Phoenix says soberly, and I nod in concurrence. We quickly walk through the doorway, not daring to look back. This is one memory I'm happy to leave behind for good.

18

I step onto the gym floor of my junior high auditorium with at least half of my grade sitting in the stands. My palm meets my face as I recognize the scene before me. I'd better keep my guard up because right now, I'm receiving some major blows riding on this memory train.

"Is this one of your pep rally days?" Phoenix asks, slightly amused.

I push my thick, black curls from my face, cringing at the familiar embarrassment that I'm now about to relive. I answer him, "Yes, that's exactly what this was. It's also the most embarrassing day of my life. I had to learn the hard way to never dive headfirst."

Through the gym doors comes a naïve, fourteen-year-old version of me. My skin tone has darkened to the caramel tone I hold now, and my ebony hair was pressed straight and parted down the middle, stopping just above my shoulders. I also realize how shapely I was when I was just starting to develop. No wonder my mom always bought me long, thick shirts.

I watch my teenage self walk to the center of the gym, where the assistant principal is standing. Next to him is a folding table that has student honor certificates, red, white, and blue ribbons, and various awards and prizes. The assistant principal grabs the wireless microphone from the table and begins fidgeting with it until it turns on, letting out ear-crushing feedback. A few classmates let out foul words, distracting the ceremony.

The assistant principal speaks into the mic. "Quiet down, class from hell! You should be ashamed that only a third of your class can make honor roll or show up to class every damn day! You get your cookies and punch at the end of the award ceremony. I want you all to welcome your fellow honor roll classmate, Ms. Cadence Queen. She's going to be singing the national anthem. Give her a warm welcome."

A few students clap as teenage me takes the microphone and closes her eyes. I wince, awaiting the moment that took years of self-esteem away. I look at my teenage self, standing confidently with her head held high and chin toward the sky. That teen girl closes her eyes, opens up, and sings softly, "Oh say, can you see..."

Then nothing else comes out but silence. I watch myself choke on the words that represent our great nation in front of a bunch of teenagers. Since this happened my freshman year of high school, my reputation didn't really precede me afterward.

Teenage me opens her eyes in a look of shock and revolt. All the kids in the gym begin booing and yelling insults. I watch my crushed self race out of the gym, remembering how I had wished to die back then. The gym doorway lights up as the angry, misunderstood, teenage version of me runs out of school that day and walks an hour and a half home just so no one would see me cry.

"Damn, Cadence. I don't know how you lived through that. Did you get picked on a lot?" Phoenix asks, concerned.

I answer him, "Not really like you would think. No one ever took my singing seriously again, though. After this, I got really into rock music and dressing in punk clothes. Even though I should have and wanted to quit music after this, I couldn't. I discovered that the one thing that was going to help me overcome everything is music. So, I kept singing, but I realized that I had a long road of learning ahead of me."

"I must admit that I'm intrigued by your life, Cadence. I've never met anyone like you, alive or dead," Phoenix speaks sincerely.

I begin walking toward the door, smirking at his words. I say to him, "Yeah, you're in for a real treat." He chuckles, and I can feel his footsteps behind me as we walk through the gym doors, taking us to the next page of my life story.

✳ ✳ ✳

We step into the old house that I lived in throughout the duration of my high school years. We moved around a lot, but eventually settled down here, and it gave me some stability. Stability literally comes with a cost.

I walk into the living room, remembering the African artwork hanging on beige painted walls and the matching leather furniture that once had a place in my life. I used to feel hate and resentment for this place. It was a nice home for a middle-class family, and I was grateful to have one, but we couldn't afford it no matter how hard we worked.

"This place was considered a step up for us, but in reality, in nearly sank us. Plus, the economy crashed, and the housing market went downhill. That left us struggling and still with no father around to care. No one was there to help us stay above water, and before we knew it, we were drowning in a deep ocean called debt," I say.

Eighteen-year-old me walks into the living room. My small, hourglass frame fits into black, ripped jeans with a dog chain hooked on my belt buckle and a black tank top, accessorized with a skull design purse hanging on my right shoulder.

My hair is straightened, and my bangs cover my left eye—a look I wore because I thought it made me look extra mysterious. I can't help but giggle to myself at how dramatic I was. My demeanor is that of a tough, badass chick not to be messed with, but in reality, I was just a little girl trying to find a place to belong.

Eighteen-year-old me walks out of the front door with her car keys, ready to get going. Moments later, she frantically rushes back inside, digging inside of her purse until she finds her cell phone. I watch myself dial my mother to ask her what's going on.

The other me speaks into the phone, "Mom! My car is missing! It's just gone from the driveway. Someone must have stolen it!"

I watch the other me listening, and I can't help but shake my head at it all, already knowing the outcome. I keep quiet and watch myself. Younger me is freaking out and pacing in circles, listening to the conversation. She lets out a cry and quickly covers her mouth, muffling herself. Or should I say myself?

The other me nods and speaks. "Okay, so long story short: you gave my car up. Mom, I work fulltime. How am I supposed to get around? That car was paid for; why would you sell it? Can we at least get our stuff out of the car? I had a lot—"

She listens for a moment before speaking angrily into the phone, "Mom, all of my lyrics and music equipment were in the trunk! I have to at least get my songs back; that's my property. They can't keep my property—they can't. See, you don't even care. Fine. I'm eighteen, so stop caring, but I'm done. I am sick of working all the time to have everything taken from me anyway. I'm moving out." Former me hangs up the phone and walks into the back room, screaming all the way there, lighting the doorway behind her.

"I can't believe that happened," Phoenix says.

"I was angry at her for a long time. The older I got, the more I understood how hard it is in the world when you're alone. I loved my mom, and I know she did her best, but I had to make my own way. I couldn't accept that this was all there would be for me—that I was just going to be another cliché. Black women get stereotyped as difficult loud mouths, but no one ever stops to wonder why. Maybe it's because no one listens!

But when I sang, people finally heard me. They listened," I reveal emotively.

"I hear you," Phoenix says. "I think you're brave, Cadence. Most people don't get to follow their dreams or even figure out what their dreams are. You've gone through some brutal, vile tests, but you got through it. Did you get a chance to get your music out there?"

I laugh at his question, knowing that he's seen my lows, but not my highs. I reply, "Oh, yeah. I got my music out there, alright. One quality I always cherished about myself was that I'm a woman of my word."

Phoenix raises his eyebrow, crossing his arms and giving me a lopsided grin. "Well that's a great quality for a Queen."

I laugh at him playfully referencing my name. He waits for me to walk toward the door before following behind me.

Suddenly, I feel a sense of relief knowing that the worst is behind me, and I am moving forward to the better parts of my life before the ultimate downfall. No gust of wind available for me, unfortunately; if I want my canoe to move, I have to row myself.

19

We cross to the other side, finding ourselves on a basement stairway I know too well. This dimly lit stairway belonged to my drummer. He was the oldest and had the most stable income, so he could afford to insulate his basement, so we could jam out worry-free. I can hear the loud electric guitar strumming random chords, getting warmed up to play. I can hear my drummer beating on his set, doing a sound check.

Phoenix smiles, asking, "Is this your band?"

"Yes," I reply, smiling and headbanging to the sounds.

"Let's check it out. It's sounding cool," Phoenix says.

We walk down the steps, turn the corner, and there I am, a twenty-one-year-old girl wearing her server outfit, or whatever restaurant job I was working at the time. There I am, mic in my hand, swaying back and forth to the music, getting ready for the time change for me to begin singing. A surge of emotive energy rushes through me as I relive this day. This was our first band practice together, put together by our rhythm guitarist and my eventual fiancé, Jim.

I watch him swaying his guitar around, lost inside the melody, anxiously waiting for my performance. I had been answering ads for bands seeking lead singers for about a year before a musician friend introduced me to Jim, who was a rhythm guitarist looking for a lead singer to complete his band. We exchanged numbers, had this practice, and everything just took off from there.

I watch his green eyes focus on my past self when my part begins, and a cheeky smile soon follows. My other self closes her eyes and begins singing with her melodic, powerful voice:

Verse:
If every human has a heart,
Why do I see nothing, a blank stare on your face?
If every living thing has to move,
Why do you stand so still, frozen in place?
Chorus:
You're, dead to me!
You are! Dead to me!

You're, dead to me!
You are! Dead to me!
Verse:
If every human needs to breathe,
Why do I stand by, watching you suffocating?
If every living thing needs to feed,
Why do you starve your mind of all that you need?
Chorus:
You're, dead to me!
You are! Dead to me!
You're, dead to me!
You are! Dead to me!
Bridge:
You may be alive, but you're not living!
You may be alive, but life is unforgiving!
You may be alive, but you're not living!
You may be alive, but death is unforgiving!

The band transitions to the solo, and everyone goes wild except me; I'm just listening and keeping time. As I continue listening, the lyrics start to become eerie. I look at Phoenix, and he's completely transfixed by the song and us jamming out. A drumstick slips out of my drummer's hand, landing right next to my own feet. He quickly grabs another stick without losing a beat, progressing along with the song. The lead guitarist plays that last guitar lick before returning to the verse.

Verse:
If every human being needs a home,
Why do you live empty, so alone?
If every living thing must grow,
Why do you wilt and decay six feet below?

Those words are stabbing me inside right now. I named this song "Dead to Me," because I thought it was a fun, in-your-face song to sing about, especially to ex-lovers. Now this song means something else entirely.

Chorus:
You're, dead to me!
You are! Dead to me!
You're, dead to me!
You are! Dead to me!
Bridge:
You're dead to me!
You've already died!
You're dead to me!
You've already tried!
You're dead to me!
There is nothing inside!

The song ends abruptly, creating an awkward silence. "Damn, that song is badass! Cadence, where did you learn to write like that?" my enthusiastic bass player asks, while doing runs on his fretless bass guitar. He always played effortlessly. Everyone in my band was insanely talented, and they helped me become better. They helped as best as they could, at least.

Jim interjects, "You don't learn how to become a singer-songwriter; either you're born one or you're not, and Cadence, you are one. Guys, what do you think? I think we struck gold here, but I know we have to vote. I vote Cadence to be in the band. I think she's the one." Jim looks at past me and winks before turning his attention back to the band.

My drummer, Derek, votes yes while adjusting his drum kit. My bass player and lead guitarist—both named Chris, which was always fun confusing the two—stepped up and said yes as well.

"Okay, we have our new lead singer, and now our band is complete! We are now Pipe Dreams!" Jim yells excitedly.

"All hail the Queen!" my drummer shouts, poking at my last name. My bandmates are in on the joke, laughing aloud while I wear the happiest smile I had ever seen myself make.

Jim positions his guitar and begins playing the riff and singing the song "God Save the Queen" by the Sex Pistols, and the jokes really begin. I catch myself laughing at the scene, remembering how happy I was and how meeting them changed my life. This band was literally the best thing that ever happened to me, and I sabotaged it. I would give anything to be back there singing with my bandmates, lost in Jim's presence. I can't do that because I'm just as stupid as I am smart. A mean elementary school teacher told me that once, and for the first time, I understand what she meant.

Phoenix taps my shoulder, alerting me of the glowing doorway awaiting, right above us. We walk back up the stairs and pass through the light, and for the first time, I didn't want to leave. I know I must keep moving forward, though. If this were a mountain, then I'm just now reaching the summit, I suppose.

* * *

We get transported to a botanical garden. A plethora of plants and flowers mirroring every color of the rainbow that spreads down a trail that extends for miles. Off into the distance, I recognize the rose garden I used to visit. The botanical garden was one of my favorite hot spots. It was always quiet and clean and full of exquisite, hard-earned, natural beauty. Being around nature is one of the few places where I could ground myself and find harmony.

I walk toward the rose garden, and Phoenix follows closely. He asks, "This place is beautiful; did you get married here or something?"

I chuckle, answering, "No, I just love botanical gardens because, well, what's not to love? I would have loved that, though."

I let out a heavy sigh as we come closer to the rose garden, and I see past me having a picnic with Jim inside my favorite spot, that beautiful, white gazebo. He's doodling around on his acoustic guitar, and I'm laughing at something he's saying. Jim reaches his hand out, aiming for my hair, but I swat his hand away, laughing.

We had this ineffable vibe that couldn't keep us away from each other. Despite our opposite cultures, we shared the same dream, and our paths seemed destined to be together. I never stopped loving him, but I stopped showing it, which led to a lot of problems. Right in this moment, I couldn't think of a single thing I would have rather been doing than spending the day with him.

Phoenix clears his throat before awkwardly asking, "So were you and your guitar player dating?"

"It was so much more than dating. I was reluctant at first because he was my bandmate and thought it would complicate things, but I couldn't resist his spell for very long. For the first time in my life, I had a guy who understood me and loved me as I was. Just being there was enough for him, and he went out of his way to make sure I was happy. I couldn't have asked for a better partner in life," I answer honestly, feeling my words stabbing my wounded heart.

"What happened to you guys? What tore you apart?" Phoenix asks, intrigued.

"You'll see; that I'm sure of. At the end of the day, we're all just victims of our circumstances."

A bright light bursts inside the gazebo, swallowing the fond memory of my date and disappearing forever. Now it's time to move on to what's next. I really took for granted how disposable life really is, and that nothing lasts forever. I walk inside the gazebo one last time without saying a word. I close my eyes and let the light engulf me, embracing its warmth and accepting what I can't get back.

* * *

The light dissipates. I open my eyes only to be met with camera flashes and a spotlight shining right above my former self posing with my band. I look around and notice people are standing around, conversing and drinking while watching us pose.

My manager steps in front of us holding our platinum album in the air and speaks. "This is what happens when you believe in Pipe Dreams, everyone! So much to celebrate! I'm so happy that I was lucky enough to find this special band. You watch: Pipe Dreams are taking over the world!"

People in the room clap and cheer, and my bandmates and I are all hugging each other, grateful yet basking in our hard-earned achievement. Phoenix appears next to me, and I look at him, ready to fill him in. He's immediately drawn to my band, watching us mingle happily among our business associates and fans.

"So, is this one of those album release parties?" he asks, placing his hands on his hips.

I reply, "No. We were celebrating our album going platinum. We were this alternative rock band, and the label didn't have a lot of faith in us, so we had a lot to prove, and we did. Our debut album ended up going triple platinum between ten countries. We toured all of those countries, and we suddenly found that our pipe dreams became our reality."

I turn to look at my old self. During this time, I thought I had become everything I had set out to be. I was unbreakable, and I finally had everything I ever wanted. I was just reaching my mid-twenties, petite, with an athletic build and glowing, caramel skin tone. My frame was always small, but shapely, and by the time I became a success, I had finally become comfortable with my sex appeal. I knew what I was doing wearing that crimson red dress that night, with the gold pumps and lipstick just a shade darker than my outfit.

Jim walks into the center of the room and begins clinking beer bottles together, getting everyone's attention. He's not drunk—far from it. He looks dashing, wearing his navy blue, two-piece suit with a black dress shirt and shoes. His freshly shaven face holds that genuine, warm smile that became the first thing I fell in love with. Whenever he smiled at me, with his mesmerizing green eyes that glistened like emeralds, I would feel so conflicted. His smile made me feel safe and grounded, but his eyes would get me lost, and I would lose control.

Jim speaks. "Excuse me, everyone. Thank you all so much for the love and support. This has been the wildest ride for all of us, and we don't take any of this for granted." Jim places the bottles on the floor and continues. "Cadence, sweetheart, where are you? I can't finish this speech without the guest of honor!" he shouts excitedly.

The other me appears from the small crowd and walks to the center of the room, meeting Jim. There is a trail of whistling, clapping, and cheers as my past self-confidently carries herself around the room. Jim, still smiling, grabs my hand and kisses it softly. I can see my bandmates gathering around, trying to keep their cool, but I know they know. He speaks again. "Wow. You just... You look so beautiful, Cadence. You're the best thing that has ever happened to me, and you always believed that I was a good man and that I could continue to be better. When I'm with you, everything in my existence is better, and I can't know what living without you feels like."

By this time, I have an idea of what he's going to ask. I feel a tear slipping from my right eye. Jim reaches in his pocket and pulls out that little black box that means everything. I remember feeling my entire body freeze, and for a moment, it was like I forgot how to breathe voluntarily. My mind was too busy to involve my involuntary function. Jim gets down on one knee, looks me in my eyes, and holds the box up in front of me.

He speaks. "Cadence, will you keep making me a better man and marry me?"

Past me covers her mouth, fighting back the tears before answering, "Yes! Yes, I will marry you! I've loved you from day one!"

Jim laughs, removes the ring from the box, and places it on my ring finger. The ring was perfect: a sapphire gem, which represented my birthstone, that had specks of diamonds decorated around it. It was a perfect fit, and I never took it off until the day I killed myself. This was the happiest day of my life. Jim is embracing past me in a passionate, exploratory kiss, and my bandmates cut in, yelling and bursting open champagne bottles.

"I don't understand, Cadence. You had made all your dreams come true. What could have been so bad that you wanted to kill yourself? Did Jim cheat on you with a groupie, or did someone die? Did someone hurt you?" Phoenix asks in a soft tone, showing me a look of concern.

I open my mouth to speak, but the ball of light appears, flying past us, across the room and into the exit door. The door lights up, creating the spiritual gateway that's eventually going to help me move on.

I look at Phoenix and say, "You'll understand soon enough."

He shrugs his shoulders and speaks. "You know you can talk to me. I'm here because I want to help you though this."

I reply, "I know. I'm not trying to shut you out, it's just hard to talk about it, and I know it's coming up anyway. It made too big of an impact on my life." I say

"It's okay. I'm here, and we'll get through it together. I promise," Phoenix says.

I give him a gratified, closed-lipped smile, and he pats me on the back. We turn and begin walking to the next flashback of my complex, unconventional life.

20

We reach the other side, stepping onto a stage. My entire band is on stage experimenting with their instruments, except me. I always entered the stage last; it was part of the diva vibe I had going whenever I performed. I look toward the audience and recognize this show. Thousands of people crammed together in this stadium, all there to see the main act: us. This was the last show during our first headlining tour, and it was the biggest show we had ever played.

We liked to incorporate space themes for our live shows. Our stage background was a space design filled with a beautiful golden hue nebula with shining stars and stardust surrounding it. The spotlight gleamed toward the center of the stage, anticipating my arrival.

Our band name, Pipe Dreams, is lit up in the center with a grand look. The crowd is screaming our band name in random, incoherent shouts, and you literally feel the wave of energy the crowd is sending out. My drummer is practicing rolls on his set, my bass player is fingering away, and both guitar players are harmonizing their licks, awaiting my presence.

I look at Phoenix and say, "This was probably the best show we've ever played. It was our first headlining tour, and it was our show. We got to be the main event, and it was amazing. I was living in a rock n roll fairy tale. I thought nothing could touch me, but I was wrong—very wrong."

"What's the name of this song?" Phoenix asks.

I open my mouth to speak, but I stop when I see my past self strutting on stage. I'm dressed in my signature, purple cocktail dress that I accessorized with black leather gloves and boots. I also had on a yin yang necklace that I had bought in a Wicca store in Colorado. It had literally fallen into my hands as I touched the rack to check the price tag on a different item. The owner said that it was a synchronicity, and that I was meant to have it. It went in one ear and out of the other, but I did buy it. I liked what it meant; it felt representative of Jim and me.

It eventually inspired me to write this song. Past me shines with a twinkle in her eye and excitement in her gut, ready to pour her heart and soul out using the rare gift she was given. The gift that everyone in the crowd is screaming, shouting, and begging for. All the pain, disappointments, insecurities, hate, and fear disintegrates into oblivion, my spirit breaks free, and in this moment, I became bodiless. Singing was my super power, and the fact that I got to do it for a living was the best feeling in the world. It was as good as flying, but when you fly, it's inevitable that one day you will fall.

"It's called 'Yin Yang.' I wrote it for my love, Jim," I reveal, trying to hide my despair.

The song begins with a lead guitar intro playing two measures, then the entire band joins in and plays two more measures before the former me opens her mouth and releases the song inside of her:

Verse:
I push, you pull, I burn, you cool.
You give, I take, you love, I hate!
I'm wrong, you're right, I'm dark, you're light.
You're fast, I'm slow, you stop, I go!
Chorus:
Yin yang, yin yang.
Yin yang, yin yang!
Verse:
I fall, you rise, I'm earth, your sky.
You're up, I'm down, you smile, I frown!
I'm silent, you're sound, I'm lost, you're found.

You're right, I'm left, your birth, I'm death!
Chorus:
Yin yang, yin yang.
Yin yang, yin yang!
Bridge:
Feed off me, and I'll feed off you!
Oppose me, challenge everything I do!
Feed off me, and I'll feed off you!
We'll come together, form into something new!

The song transitions to the melodic guitar solo that builds into a captivating performance. The beautiful chaos we were projecting had everyone mesmerized, and I, myself, get lost in the music, forgetting the world around me. The music transitions back to the intro, playing two measures before entering the next verse.

Verse:
I walk, you fly, I'm wet, your dry.
You're front, I'm back, you yield, I attack!
I'm free, you're paid, I'm night, your day.
You're virtue, I'm sin, you're yang, I'm!
Chorus:
Yin yang, yin yang.
Yin yang, yin yang!

The band finishes the song by banging their instruments, improvising crazy, chaotic, intricate sounds crashing together. The crowd is cheering with their hands in the air, reaching out to us. I can still remember that euphoric, aching feeling in my chest after each song. The energy from all those beautiful souls screaming for more is everything—just beautifully unifying. This moment was the pinnacle of my human experience. I had felt the sensation of flying, and I thought I had become invincible. The pride comes before the fall, like the calm before the storm.

The ball of light flies through the stage curtain, leading toward the backstage. My stomach drops upon this sight, my sunny memories are gone, and it's back to the storm.

* * *

We walk through the curtain and find ourselves standing in a hotel parking lot during nightfall.

Suddenly, I can hear my own heartbeat drumming in my ears in rising fright. I take a step back, attempting to turn around, but I'm stopped by a sharp pain in my stomach. It's as if I've been hit by a wrecking ball. I had everything arranged perfectly in my house, and one day, without warning, an unstoppable force had burst through my walls, and just like that, my whole life changed forever.

"Hey, are you okay?" Phoenix asks.

I sigh heavily before lifting my head to speak. I see my tour bus parked in the back corner of the parking lot. I put my hand over my mouth, muting the sounds of my escaping sobs. I see my old self walking on the hotel's second floor toward the stairs, holding an ice bucket. I begin shaking my head as I watch my old self walk down those stairs, around the corner, and into the vending area.

"I can't do this!" I exclaim, turning away from Phoenix in shame.

I can hear him stepping closer as he says, "Hey, it's okay. Just try to stay calm. Tell me what's wrong."

My lips begin quivering, and my breathing becomes heavier. I take a long, deep breath before answering, "I can't watch myself get raped again. I just want it to fucking go away!"

Phoenix's jaw drops, flabbergasted at my confession. He walks up to me and grabs my shoulders in consolation, and I feel the sensation of compassion. I close my eyes to avoid his blue gaze, but I quickly give in, realizing I've already done the hard part of revealing my internal hardship.

He speaks. "Cadence, you know we have no choice. We have to keep moving on. Think about it like this: this is the very last time you will ever have to relive it. One more time, let this time be one that makes you stronger."

I back away from his loose grip as his words resonant with me. He's right. I spent all of my time trying to forget it ever happened, but this time was different. A drunken man who I had never laid eyes on before this night violated my body and threatened my life. I, the touring rock star on my way to world domination, still somehow ended up at the wrong place at the wrong time. It was a foreign pain that I had never felt before, and it changed me. It was a whole new suffering for me.

"You're right," I reply. "I need to finally get past this. I can't harbor it any longer."

"There's the strong woman I know," Phoenix jokes, making me grin.

I start walking toward the vending area where it all happened, and Phoenix follows suit. As we're walking, he asks me, "So why were you staying at a hotel like this if you guys were making millions of dollars?"

I laugh, replying, "We were not millionaires. Record labels always make their money first. We sold well, which meant we could keep our deal. This was our last night on the road before we were to fly back to headquarters and renegotiate our contract. We took a small deal, and the label was thrilled that we sold more than expected. We were going to get full creative control of our music, and the stars were finally aligned. I never had any problems as long as the hotel was clean and safe. I never would have stayed here if I had known that rapists roamed the area. Regardless, here we are."

"Regardless, it wasn't your fault. It's never the victim's fault. I hope you know that," Phoenix says.

"I know," I answer somberly.

We reach the enclosed vending area, and its entrance is glowing vibrantly, as if it were awaiting our arrival. We walk through the next tragic door of my life, and I'm not certain of what the outcome will be. I hope I'm capable of finally putting the past to rest and get to a place where I can finally find peace within myself. Whether I reach heaven, nirvana, or become reincarnated into an owl, I'll never know if I don't face my fears.

We walk into the familiar vending area—the place that would terrorize my life until its very end. Looking at it from the outside, there is nothing scary at all about this room. One side of the room has the vending machines placed on the edge of the wall. A large ice machine was on the other side, along with trash cans, leaving little space between.

Past me walks in holding an empty ice bucket in her hand with the bruised arm from a hard fall during a gig that previous night. She's wearing a simple, white tank top and black shorts. Her long, thick curls are balled into a bun, and she has a large set of headphones on, oblivious to the world around her. She stops by the ice machine to fill up her bucket. She finishes and heads to the exit, but stops suddenly, noticing the snack machine on the other side. I watch the past unfold in front of me, as past me caves into her desires and fatefully walks over to get a snack instead of just going back to her room.

The blood in my veins begins boiling as I remember that disgusting monster. He reeked of stale cigarettes, liquor, and garbage, like that's what he worked around. A thousand flowers could never mask that smell, a thousand showers could never wash that filth away, and a thousand therapies could never make me forget that I was raped. Anger sets off inside of me like a bomb, and before I know it, I'm running toward the exit.

"I can't do this! I can't!" I yell.

"Cadence, no!" Phoenix screams, racing after me. He speeds in front of me, preventing me from exiting.

My arm reaches out for the exit, and when it crosses the other side of the doorway, it turns gray, just like Craig.

"No! No! Their making me stay! I can't watch this, Phoenix! I can't do this! The first time already felt like a sick joke, but this is worse!" I cry in despair. I yank my arm back inside, and it's still gray. It feels twice as heavy and so stiff that I can barely move my fingers.

"You have to stay, Cadence. You know what will happen if you don't. You're better than all this. So much stronger than this. What did you do before when life got you down? When it got too hard?"

Phoenix asks, eyes staring in mine as if he were conjuring the vulnerability right out of me.

"I sang," I say, chuckling at the thought while clearing away the tears coming down my face.

"Well, sing. If you sing while you face the pain head on, it will keep you strong enough to fight it. You have to face it, Cadence; no more running. That's how we got here in the first place," Phoenix says before pulling me into an embrace. I nod my head while pressed against his chest, hearing his words in my head like a song on repeat.

Just as we part, the monster walks in. Well, no monster really—just a man. He's stands in the doorway wearing black coveralls and a matching beanie with no logo printed on it. I look down at his muddy, steel-toed boots, then back up to his large exterior, and I shake my head. He takes his first step into the room, and I react by shutting my eyes.

I try to think of a song to sing that held me in the dark before. I remember that my favorite song to sing was called "Come Angel." I could never remember who sang it, but it spoke to me. It always lifted my spirits and made me feel better about myself. The melodic, melancholy style in which it was sang was what captured me the most.

The man walks over to past me, who is still at the vending machine deciding on a snack while listening to music, unaware of a presence in the room. The old me is preparing to put the dollar into the machine, but before she can, the man forcibly grabs her and throws her onto the ground. I watch past me scream and struggle, but I know nothing will stop this violation from happening.

My head begins spinning, and I feel like I'm about to puke and pass out from this scene unfolding. Instead, I raise my head up, find that song inside of me, and open my mouth to release the pain of this day. How it makes me feel, and how I feel to have to face it again. This time is different because as horrible as all of this is, I can at least take solace in the fact that after this time, I will never have to face it again. If I can make it, I can finally get past this and maybe finally be free of this chapter.

I subconsciously wrap my arms around myself in a defensive position. A soft melody escapes my throat, and the room is suddenly filled with my voice. I begin singing my heart out, a cappella.

Verse:

Come, angel, take me far, far away into a land of enchantment.
Come, angel, take me to a place where the wind dances with grace.
Come, angel, set me free. I'll follow the breadcrumbs to imaginary.
Chorus:
To me, there is no place like here. My troubles are gone.
No reason to fear. My obstinate nature bursts into flames,
and I bathe in salvation.
Verse:
Come, angel, save me from myself. Rid me from this anguish.
Come, angel, make me feel that I don't need pain to heal.

Come, angel, show me the way. Help me escape this
world of hate.
Come, angel, take the time to play, laughing and
crying and loving always.
Chorus:
To me, there is no place like here. My troubles are
gone.
No reason to fear. My obstinate nature bursts into
flames,
and I bathe in salvation.

As I'm singing, I look down and notice that my
arm is returning to normal as I sing each note. This sign
encourages me to keep singing my heart out.

A man runs into the room, yanking that vile man
off the past me and punching him in the face. The man
turns to the broken, violated girl that was once me,
takes off his shirt, and hands it to her, saying, "It's
okay; you're safe now."

Another man walks into the room, asking what's
going on. The drunken rapist stumbles up from the
ground and runs out of the room, lighting the doorway
behind him. The man who saved me yells, "Don't let
that son of a bitch get away! He's a rapist!"

The men run out of the room, leaving a torn up,
sobbing, helpless version of me. I look at the old me,

and the feeling of disgust and humiliation creeps back to haunt me. I don't feel so embarrassed about it now. There was nothing I could have done to stop him, and nothing I did to provoke him either. He was a drunken pervert looking to score anything he could get his hands on, and I was the unlucky prey.

"You did it," Phoenix says. "I'm proud of you, Cadence. We're both going to make it out of here, grow in some spiritual way, and find our happiness."

"Thanks," I reply, pulling him into a hug for a change. We embrace briefly, then I release myself from him. I say, "Let's get out of here. I'm closing the curtains, and I am done with this show. There's still a dim light glowing inside of me, and as long as it's there, I can't give up. I'm never giving up on anything ever again. I'm going to see everything through no matter how painful it may prove to be."

"Well after you, miss rock star," Phoenix says.

I give a warm, genuine smile that lights me up inside like I was alive. It's bittersweet to be called that, but how many people can say they were a rock star at all? Unlike most people who live an ordinary life, I lived an extraordinary one up until the end, of course. Still, I am responsible for my own path and the choices I've made. Facing my demons is the hardest thing I've ever had to do, and as lame as this sounds, it really is making me stronger. As hard as this was, I know I'm going to somehow survive it all.

So off to visit the downward spiral that came after this horrific incident. I already know what happens, but instead of dreading it like I have been, I'm going to charge in head first, ready to tackle any obstacle I have to endure. I've survived the worst of my life, but this isn't the end of it. I still have a few screw-ups to witness before I surrender to my fate. I walk through the doorway, head high and fist balled, ready for what's next.

21

We arrive at another concert venue, standing on the right side of the stage next to giant speakers while my bandmates jam around waiting to play the next song. The place is packed with people bunched together, shoving each other around waiting to get a glimpse of me. The former me is standing in the center of a purple lit stage, clutching the mic stand, head hanging low to avoid the gazes—to avoid a connection.

My lead guitarist, Chris, begins the song with a fire-eating guitar intro, hitting the airwaves like a freight train. He plays two measures before the rest of the band joins in, everyone is playing fast, aggressive sounds, producing a decibel level off the charts. Even in death, I can feel the intense vibrations my band loved creating. I feel a tingling sensation underneath my feet as each beat progresses into the first verse.

The former me finally lifts her head up, revealing a slightly dazed, apathetic frontwoman with no interest in entertaining. While waiting for the change where the vocals are supposed to enter, she turns away from the mic, belching from the alcohol she consumed before the show. She straightens up the spaghetti straps of her black dress that keep falling from her shoulders. I can barely watch this performance and barely recognize who I used to be. I once had boundless energy to jump around and prance on stage. Here, I look like I can barely stand.

I turn to Phoenix, giving him a self-conscious look, and in return, he sends me a sympathetic one. We turn back to this train wreck of a performance, and I feel agony developing in my gut. I was in a terrible place where all I felt was anger and resentment. I thought I was keeping it all together by getting on with my life and returning to the hustle and bustle of a musician's life. Thought I would find myself again once I got back to what I was good at and what people loved me for.

The truth is that when something traumatic happens in life, it changes you. You are taken away from your environment, shoved into a new one, and expected to adapt and survive. Yes, I may have survived the change, but I didn't adapt to it very well. I can't even pinpoint exactly what shut off inside of me, but I know it happened. I was closed off, and before I knew it, everything that I had worked so hard for was falling to pieces around me.

The former me sings the first verse:

Verse:
There's no telling what you think of me,
I'm awkward, and I'm a freak.
It's no telling why you talk to me,
My sarcasm doesn't hide my brutal honesty.
So why are you trying to win my heart when there is just a hole?
Chorus:
So, let me make you understand,
I don't need you helping hand,
I don't need your therapy,
All I need are the drugs in me!
Verse:
You think that dreams really come true?
Wait till you see what life does to you.
You think that love can save us all?
Well, be prepared to watch yourself fall.
You don't control anything in your life,
So, stop spreading your unwanted light.
Just go away!
Chorus:
So, let me make you understand,

I don't need you helping hand,
I don't need your therapy,
All I need are the drugs in me!
Bridge:
There's no person left to save in me; all that's left are
the drugs in me!
There's no person left to save in me; all that's left are
the drugs in me!
There's no person left to save in me; all that's left are
the drugs in me!

The lead and rhythm guitarists harmonize the solo
while the bass and drum keep the melody going.

Chorus:
So, let me make you understand,
I don't need you helping hand,
I don't need your therapy,
All I need are the drugs in me!
So, let me make you understand,
I don't need you helping hand,
I don't need your therapy,
All I need are the drugs in me!

The hard fuzz toned guitars play together in
chaos, with the bass pounding and vibrating around the

room and drum sticks beating the cymbals while crashing the snare and bass drum. The past me throws the microphone on the ground, picks up the mic stand, and begins banging it on the ground. The crowd is going wild at her destructive behavior, screaming loudly and reaching their arms out, lost in the madness.

She fails to break the mic stand after a few bangs, so she walks over to the drum kit and begins destroying it with the stand. My band stops playing, and all you hear is me yelling at each hit I give the drum while the audience applauds. The drum set is in pieces before former me snaps out of it. Breathing heavy, she finally looks up at her drummer, and he looks livid. She turns to the rest of the band, and they all appear stunned and more importantly Jim, who is shaking his head in disappointment. She drops the mic stand and bows to the crowd before taking one last look at her bandmates and walking off stage.

The backstage entrance brightens, and Phoenix turns to me and says, "That was rock and roll."

"That was a meltdown. It's also the last show I ever played, which makes it more painful to watch," I say. The realization hits me like a hurricane as I'm drowning in a sea of my downfalls. I hate that my legacy is when I was in my absolute worst place instead of my best.

"We should go," Phoenix says.

I nod and glance briefly at the now empty stage with a bittersweet feeling; bitter because this was my worst performance, and sweet because for a moment in time, I got to live my pipe dream. It may not have worked out the way I wanted, but I had made it. I had tasted the fruit of the success tree and got to travel to foreign lands that sang my songs word for word. I watched people sing my songs in jubilation, praising my emotions as their own and reminding me of the connection we all have between us. Making me feel my humanity again.

22

We walk through the light, entering the other side. The first thing I notice is that I'm in my apartment, where I died. I can see my past self sitting on the couch smoking a joint and sipping on wine. I look at her, and it's as if I'm looking at a doppelganger. Same clothes, same hairstyle, same petite, hollow frame. For the first time, I'm really looking at myself from rock bottom, and I hate what I see.

My skin has lost its glow, my hair has lost its shine, and I'm as skinny as I can be. I wasn't taking care of myself properly, and I didn't care to. Everything that I could have been was decided in this moment, and I let myself down.

The doorbell rings, and past me yells, "Who is it?" before taking another sip of wine.

"It's Jim and the band!" Jim yells through the door.

"Hold on!" She yells, setting the wine on a coaster and putting the joint in her mouth. She gets up from the couch to unlock the deadbolt. She opens the door, and her bandmates welcome themselves inside. My former self takes another hit before plopping herself back on to the couch, exhaling the smoke from her lungs as she lands.

"So, what's this about? I never hear from you guys on a Sunday when we're not touring. Except for Jim, of course," she says nonchalantly.

I watch Jim snatch the joint out of her hands before responding. "Cadence, we're here for a band discussion."

Former me lifts her eyebrow, giving him the "What's your problem?" look. She crosses her arms and replies, "Okay, fine. What do you want to discuss?"

My drummer, Derek, speaks first. "Well, Cadence, we know things have been difficult lately. You've been acting different, and we just want to make sure you're taking care of yourself. If you need to take a break and see someone, we are fine with that. We care about you first; the band can't go on if you're not in a proper state to participate. We love you, and we're not going anywhere. We just think that it's time for you to consider other alternatives of coping."

I remember getting immediately defensive at his comment. It was obvious that I had a problem, but I was so emotionally weak, and when I'm in that condition, it's like my soul tunes out and my ego steps in. Former me steps away from her bandmates, arms still crossed in attempt to conceal the shakes that were developing. The shakes were mostly due to the conversation, but also because of drug withdrawals.

Past Cadence speaks. "So, are you asking if I want to take a break, or telling me I am?"

Jim lets out a frustrated sigh and responds. "We are telling you that we are officially on hiatus until you get the help you need. You know you can't keep going on like this, Cadence."

Cadence chuckles condescendingly before replying, "You can't just vote on something without consulting me; I'm your damn singer. I'm working out my problems. Once this trial is over and that bastard gets sentenced, I'll get cleaned up. But I can't quit singing until then. We're not canceling this tour."

My guitar player, Chris, speaks. "Cadence, the majority rules. You don't decide for all of us; you know that. This is for the best. Give yourself a break; you've been through a terrible trauma, and you need to take care of yourself. After this last show, we're more certain than ever that you're subconsciously crying for help."

"Help? No, I'm managing just fine, thank you. We haven't had to cancel any shows yet, so I don't understand what I'm doing wrong," Cadence replies.

"You massacred my favorite drum set! My dad worked overtime for two months to get me that set! It should have died a natural death, not by you," Derek replies.

Past me scratches her head, giving an exasperated look. "I apologized for that, and I already got your replacement in the mail. I lose control one time, and suddenly, I have a problem," Cadence replies bitterly.

"We know about the cocaine," Jim retorts in distress.

I look at Phoenix, and he looks at me, flabbergasted. His facial expression quickly changes into a look of concern. I turn away from his gaze, feeling a tinge of shame as he watches my downward spiral unfold. I watch the former me getting called out and her feelings getting hurt in the process.

Past Cadence jaw drops before saying, "You told them!"

"I'm sorry, Cadence, but you broke my drum set. It went too far, and you never quit like you promised me. You broke your promise too," Derek replies defensively.

Cadence shrugs her shoulders indifferently, raising her arms up in the process. She speaks. "Well, I guess we're even now."

Jim replies to her, "He's not to blame for all of this—you are. You are making a choice to hurt yourself, and it's hurting the band. You know we wouldn't be here if we didn't love you. You're going to be my wife, Cadence. You know I feel like I'm being slapped in the face every time you choose drugs over talking to the band. Talking to me."

Cadence interrupts angrily, "You feel slapped? Try feeling broken inside. Try feeling crying tremors, incessant flashbacks of the most humiliating moment of your existence, and having to keep it all together because the show must go on! A white man raped me, and the most he'll get is a few months because that's our fucked-up justice system! Not even my growing fame can change that because I'm just another nigga to the law! Just another nobody! There's nothing any therapist can say that can change what happened to me. As far as the drugs go, it's all I have keeping me going right now. If I went to a shrink, they would just prescribe me PTSD medicine and send me on my way. What's the difference between their drugs and mine?"

"Cocaine can kill you! It can kill your voice!" Jim shouts.

"Too much of anything can kill you. Can we wrap this up? My head is starting to spin," past Cadence says imprudently, before taking another sip of her wine.

Jim speaks to her genuinely. "I don't know how to help you, Cadence. I already feel like I've failed you. I would give anything for a time machine to go back and change what happened, but I can't. I'm not going to sit back and let you destroy what you've worked so hard for because of this fucking tragedy. Please get help. You don't have to see a therapist if it makes you uncomfortable. You need to go to rehab, though. You're addicted to a drug that can kill you if you overdo it. I know you think that the drugs are helping you cope, but really, you're just addicted to the escape. You can't run away from the pain; you gotta face it head on, then you'll begin to heal."

"Okay. I'll go to rehab, but after the tour," past Cadence says, giving in.

"No, you can't wait on this. We need to get the jump on this now while you're still in your early stages of usage," Jim replies.

"I don't care. You want me to go to rehab, you got to let me get through this tour. We got a deal?" past Cadence asks, picking up her wine and taking a sip.

Jim grabs the wine glass from her and replies, "No, we don't have a deal. Either you go to rehab, or the band is done! We're not touring or doing anything else until you clean up. You got young girls that idolize you. I know you don't want them to see you at your worst. You're going to change the world and help bring all cultures together."

Cadence grabs the wine glass back from Jim before replying, "Our fans are the reason why I don't want to postpone this tour."

"It's ultimately up to you, Cadence. If you want the band to continue, you have to stop doing drugs. You're not the same person on drugs that we know and love. You're late for everything now, and your enthusiasm for our music has turned into apathy. I believe in you. I know you can overcome anything; it's one of the reasons I love you so much," Jim replies compassionately.

Cadence responds, "If you loved me so much, why did you let this happen to me?"

Jim gives the most heartbreaking reaction to what was just spoken. Tears well in his eyes, and he hangs his head low in shame. My bandmates give the former me a look of chagrin, and I remember instantly regretting those words. I had become an insufferable bitch and all I wanted to do was rub salt in my own wound. I never considered how hurting myself could hurt others too.

Jim hastily wipes the tears from his face and replies, "There it is. There's the truth. I'll never forgive myself for what happened to you. I'm trying to be here as best as I can, but I can't do this anymore, Cadence. You have a choice to make. It's us or drugs. Me or drugs."

My former self steps back in disbelief. I watch her pace around in circles on her cypress wooden floor, mind in contemplation as it seemed like I was deciding the fate of the world. She finally stops pacing and looks her bandmates in the eyes. She replies, "Okay, I'll stop. Tomorrow, I'll throw everything out and check myself into rehab. I'm only giving up the hard drugs, though. My wine, joints, and I have a relationship that extends far before the band."

"Fine. The wine and joints stay, but you have to check in tonight, not tomorrow. We need to jump on this," Jim conditions.

"No!" former me shouts. "You can't just spring in here and make demands. I'm working with you; now you have to work with me. I can't just drop everything. I need a day to process this and pack my things. I just need one more day."

"No, you just need one more time!" Jim snaps.

"What does it matter? I just need one more day! That's not too much to ask for since I'm pretty much agreeing to everything else," Cadence replies.

"Cadence, if you postpone it, you'll postpone it the next day and the one after until we find you dead!" Jim explains.

When he says the word "dead," I can't help but close my eyes and hide the painful stabbing feeling in my chest. The first time I heard it, it went in one ear, right out the other. Now I hear it, and it just makes me feel like shit.

The old me chuckles before saying, "You're overreacting. You know me, Jim; if I say I'm going to do something, I do it. Tomorrow, you can come over and help me dispose of my chemical romances. Right now, I need to be alone, so please give me some space."

Jim tries to grab Cadence's arm, but she yanks herself from his grip. "What are you doing?" Cadence yells defensively.

"I'm trying to save you. If you don't come with us now, you never will. What's it going to be?" Jim asks, giving my former self the ultimatum of my life.

"I don't know what else you want from me. You can't expect me to just drop everything and come with you. I don't appreciate you guys trying to force me to do something. Don't you think I've been forced enough?" Past Cadence's voice breaks as she pleads for sympathy.

Jim stares at Cadence, taking her all in as if it was the last time he was going to see her. Me. He gives another one of his defeated sighs, removes his matching yin yang necklace, and places it on the coffee table. My former self expresses a look of betrayal, eyes wide open and filling with fresh tears. Tears fill his own eyes as he begins walking toward the door.

"Jim, what the hell are you doing? Don't you dare walk away from me! None of you would be here if it weren't for me!" Cadence yells at her lover in fury.

"No. If you're not going to try, then I'm done trying. I can't watch you throw it all away," Jim says. He's standing in front of the door before he turns around and speaks, "I'm still in love with you, Cadence; that will never change."

Past me stomps her tiny feet toward Jim, removes her wedding ring, and throws it at his chest. Everyone looks shocked at her actions, and the room becomes silent. Cadence speaks. "If you're just going to leave when things get rough, I don't need you!"

Jim looks as if his insides are being ripped apart, and then he opens the door and leaves. One by one, my bandmates walk out the door, not saying a word. They give former me a look of insurmountable disappointment before they exit, leaving her all alone. Just before the last member shuts the door behind him, past Cadence screams, "You guys will be back!

We wouldn't be here if it weren't for my voice and my songwriting, and you know it! I brought this band to life, damn it! Go ahead; I can just be a solo artist! I don't fucking need you!"

The door slams, and it's only my ghost, Phoenix, and me, and the room grows quiet. I inhale deeply, relieved that this painful argument has finally ended, but now I must deal with what's coming next. I feel Phoenix's hand on my shoulder, giving me a meager feeling of solace. I open my eyes and look at myself—past Cadence—feeling a mixture of shock and anguish. My emotions were all over the place, and I had taken many types of drugs that deluded my thoughts. Looking at it now, it wasn't that serious. We just had a gut-wrenching fight, but I'd already survived worst. I blew up and overreacted, but in my mind, my world had officially ended.

Past Cadence picks up the wine glass and throws it at the wall, screaming as the glass shatters into pieces. She walks over to the wall mirror and gazes at her reflection.

I feel so abandoned. I can't live like this. I kill everything I touch. I'm better off dead. This is what was going through my mind in that moment. It's an awful feeling looking in the mirror and feeling repulsed at what you see.

"I know you blame yourself for what happened to the band, but I don't think they were kicking you out," Phoenix says honestly.

"I know that now. I wasn't seeing things in the right perspective. The world hurt me, and everyone I loved had left me alone. That thought sank inside of me like quicksand and became all I believed. If I couldn't play music or be with Jim, then what was the point? Death was my escape route, and it was the wrong path. I just couldn't deal with all the shame. Life was just a big joke at that point. It's not an excuse; it's just the truth," I reveal to Phoenix, turning back to the scene that led me to this point.

Past Cadence walks into her bedroom and comes out holding a black, lacquer box. She sits on the couch and places the box on the table. She lifts the lid and takes out a plastic bag with a white ball, a needle, and a tourniquet. I watch my former self take out a pre-rolled joint, grab a Zippo lighter, set fire to the plant, and inhale the smoke deeply.

I hug myself, watching my past self behave like a junkie. "I'm so embarrassed," I confess to Phoenix. The former me turns on the stereo before Phoenix could speak. An alternative rock song blares out of the speakers from a band that I'm unfamiliar with.

Past Cadence picks up a silver spoon from her box and places the white ball onto it. I watch myself cook the drug that would be my last.

Phoenix looks to me and asks, "What were you taking that needed to be cooked?"

"That was called a speedball. It's a hybrid of heroin and cocaine."

"Shit!" Phoenix blurts in surprise.

"Yeah, I got it from a dealer who hooked me up with a sample. I never planned to touch it, but for some reason, I couldn't bring myself to throw it away. Maybe deep down, I wanted an excuse to chase the high—to chase death," I say regretfully.

I turn back to my past self, and she's already got the tourniquet wrapped around her left arm. She then pierces the vein with the needle before injecting her body with the fatal chemicals. The needle is out of her arm, and she feels the effects almost instantaneously. She rips the tourniquet off her arm and stands up from the couch. The song ends, then there's a moment of silence before the next song plays.

23

The next song begins, and to my surprise, it's one of my band's songs. My song playing on the radio. *How poetic*, I remember thinking. Past Cadence grabs her joint and begins twirling around the living room, lost in a manufactured high, closing the door to reality.

This song begins with a smooth bass line that lays the melody of an alternative rock ballad. The drums, rhythm and lead guitars enter after one measure from the bass, and they all come together, transitioning gracefully. This song was always one of my personal favorites. Everyone's instruments shine radiantly, each with their own unique sound that manages to find unison. My vocals are about to start, and I tremble, feeling haunted by this memory.

Past me begins singing along to her own song, "Cure," slightly off-key, but still managing to capture the correct words. Even in all my sorrows, I still had my voice.

Verse:

You're my cure, I need you to survive.

You're so pure, I want to drink you dry.

Feel you from inside, to find, your divine powers.

Chorus:

If you are death, then I can't wait to die.

Lift my soul, sky high!

If you are love, I can't wait to fall,

Fall in between time!

If you are death, then I can't wait to die.

Lift my soul, sky high!

If you are love, I can't wait to fall,

Fall in between time!

Bridge:

This affliction is spreading. Can you cure me?

Don't know where it's heading,

Please cure me.

Verse:

You're my cure; I need you to revive.

You're so sure, you're the shining star through all the darkness.

I'm the shadow, you're my sun.

Together, we make the perfect oxymoron.

Chorus:

If you are death, then I can't wait to die.

Lift my soul, sky high!
If you are love, I can't wait to fall,
fall in between time!
If you are death, then I can't wait to die.
Lift my soul, sky high!
If you are love, I can't wait to fall,
fall in between time!
Bridge:
This affliction is spreading. Can you cure me?
Don't know where it's heading,
Please cure me.

The song goes into a breakdown where the guitars harmonize together, bass and drum hold down the melody, and the vocals disappear but return with a vengeance. I remember this moment: the moment I couldn't sing along anymore because the words are literally coming true, and I soon meet my downfall.

Verse:
My body trembles, nerves in shambles.
My vision's unclear with eyes blinded by fear.
Until you came and took my pain away!
It's love! It's love! It's love!

I watch myself collapse on the floor, hitting my head on the coffee table as I land. My last moments of life alone. I wrote this song believing that I would always choose love over death. When I felt betrayed by love, I thought death was the only cure. I understand now that suicide isn't a cure, it's a beautiful poison.

Before I know it, the song is over, and the room is quiet again. I walk over to my lifeless body, kneel on the ground, and let the tears fall. I touch the invisible barrier separating us from my human experience. "I'm so sorry; I let you down. I should have done better. I should have chosen love, not death."

Phoenix walks over and kneels beside me. He speaks. "I think it's time you forgive yourself."

I turn to him, wide-eyed, and realize he's right. It's time for me to let the past go and to make peace with everything. That's my way to absolution. I wipe my eyes and inhale deeply. "I'm done crying. I'm done feeling sorry for myself. I'm done with all of this. I forgive it all. I forgive myself. I forgive everything. I'm ready to let it all go. It's time to see what's next because I still have a lot of spiritual growing to do."

The doorway suddenly lights up, startling me upon its arrival. This is it. Everyone's fate was decided after they witnessed their death. I'm no exception to that. It's weird; I thought I would be terrified of this moment, but now that I'm here, I'm glad it's come. As painful as this has all been, at least I have closure. I know where I went right and where I went wrong, and I at least achieved my dream, even though it only lasted a moment. I'm proud of myself, and I think I can finally forgive myself for taking it all away.

I look at Phoenix and say in confidence, "I think I'm ready."

He smiles at me and says, "I'm proud of you, Cadence. I know wherever it takes us, we're going to be fine. Maybe even at peace."

We both stand up, and I say, "Thanks. I don't think I would have made it without you. You saved me."

"You saved yourself," he replies, making me gush in this moment. We turn to the doorway and slowly begin walking toward it. We step through together, light swallowing us whole and expelling us to the next place.

* * *

The light dissipates around us, and we arrive back in the void. The dreary wasteland that had become a distant memory is now my reality again. I don't see a road or anything, really. No dark ones, no river, no mountains. Before I begin to panic, I notice Phoenix's car parked right in front of us.

"What...um... What do we do now?" I ask, confused as to how I play into all of this.

He replies, laughing, "I think you know what we need to do. Are you ready?"

"No. What if we never see each other again? What if we forget each other?" I ask worriedly, suddenly unprepared to move on.

"Don't worry about any of that. We were meant to find each other, and because of that, I think we'll always have some connection. I believe that. I couldn't have chosen a better friend to walk this journey with. I'm a better person because of you, and I'll always be with you." Phoenix hugs me tighter than he's ever held me before, and I do the same.

I say, "Likewise. Thank you." Other than that, I don't know what to say. He releases me and smiles, showing his pearly whites. I laugh, ecstatic that this journey is finally ending and that I lived up to my promise. I know he's right and we'll find peace on the next side.

"Okay, it's time to go." I say, refusing to prolong our inevitable ride to the unknown. We walk to the car and get inside. I sit on the passenger's side, and Phoenix is on the driver's side.

He gives me one final smile before saying, "Goodbye, Cadence. I'll really miss you."

"I'll miss you too, Phoenix. I know that wherever you go, you'll always be a hero."

We give each other one final gaze. I take him all in, memorizing each detail so that I can remember this journey and the part he played in saving my soul. Phoenix grabs for the ignition, which has the key still inside, and turns on the car. The inside lights up, and we're suddenly blinded by it.

24

I feel a warm sensation taking over me, and I suddenly feel like my being is breaking apart. I have become the light and come into my own perfect form. My human form is only a vessel, and the real me is bodiless. I am pure energy, and I have become everything. I can't feel Phoenix's presence any longer. He must have gone his own way.

Suddenly, I feel a force pulling my light toward it. The force feels strong, but for some reason I can't explain, I feel safe where I'm going, and I surrender to it.

I travel with this force until I see a different type of light. This light is dimmer, and the closer I get to it, the heavier I feel. I reach the light, and suddenly, I'm thrown back into my human body lying in a hospital bed.

As I inhale to breathe, I begin choking, discovering a lung ventilator jammed down my throat. A nurse rushes over to me and pulls out the ventilator. When it's out, I begin coughing, wheezing, and uncontrollably crying at the same time. The nurse says to me, "It's okay. You're okay. You're okay." I begin crying even more. I'm human again. I'm alive, back in my old body. I can't believe that after everything, I'm alive.

A doctor walks into the room and over to the tray set up next to my IV. He prepares a needle, retrieves medicine from his pocket, and inserts it into my IV. It only takes a few seconds for the medicine to kick in, and even though I just woke up, I'm falling right back to sleep again.

* * *

I begin to wake up and open my eyes. I wince from a sharp pain on my frontal lobe.

"Cadence? Cadence, sweetheart, it's me," a voice says.

"Mom?" I call, turning to that familiar voice. I look over, and my mother is sitting on my right with a magazine in her hands.

She drops the magazine and grabs my hand. "It's me, baby. I'm here. Mama's right here."

Tears swell in my eyes as I begin to speak. "I'm so sorry, Mom. I didn't mean to cause you pain. I'm so sorry."

My mother squeezes my hand and wipes my tears away. "It's okay, Cadence. It's all forgiven. I'm just happy you're okay. That's all I care about. I love you, and I'm so proud of who you've become. I never dreamed you could do the things you do, and I wish I understood earlier. I have my faults too, but I promise I'm going to be here for you. You're a special person. You've inspired so many people, and you deserve the very best. You're never going to go through that suffering again. But you can't die; we need you to live."

The door opens, and Jim walks into the room. We both make eye contact, and it's like I'm seeing him for the first time. My mother gets up from her seat and moves over to the other side of the room, giving us space.

"Cadence! Cadence, you're awake! Guys, she's awake!"

Jim rushes over to my bed and stops when he reaches it. He looks into my eyes, tears in his own, and runs his hand through my hair. "I'm so happy to see your eyes open."

I touch his hand and move it closer to my face, feeling his touch and being reminded of the love we share. I know now that he and my band are all I need. "I'm so sorry for everything!"

Jim interjects, "Shh. I know. You have nothing to be forgiven for. Just promise me that you will never do anything like that again. I'm the one who found you, and it was a whole new level of pain that I never want to feel again. I'm yang and your yin, remember? Without one, the other cannot exist," he says to me, staring at me with those beautiful green eyes that I adore. He reaches in his pocket, takes out my wedding ring, and places it back on my finger.

"I'll never take it off again," I say, still crying. He smiles and gives me a peck on the lips, then on my forehead.

My bandmates walk into the room and rush over to gather around my bed. I can see all their smiling faces. My drummer, Derek, speaks first. "It's so good to see you awake. We're sorry about everything, and we love you. Everything is going to be alright now."

"Yeah, things are going to get better from now on," Jim says reassuringly.

"Have you seen the balloons and presents stacked in the room, Cadence? They're all for you, sent from fans around the world. We had to rent out a few storage units because people were sending so many gifts and get-well cards," my mother says.

I look around the room and see just that. "Get Well" and "We Love You" balloons are scattered up to the ceiling, and wrapped presents are stacked on top of each other, taking up the entire room. Jim drops a stack of fan mail as heavy as an encyclopedia on my lap.

"This is just the first stack. There are plenty more where that came from. You see how much you are loved, Cadence? Do you see how much you mean to people?" Jim says to me. He takes my other hand into his, intertwining our fingers.

I feel this overwhelming amount of love surging inside of me as I start reading a few fan cards. Each one says how much they love me and how I am their favorite singer. Fresh tears emerge again, and I cover my mouth to hold in the cries. I had no idea how many people I've impacted. People from all walks of life are inspired by my music. What a foolish girl I was to ever attempt to give all this love away.

"I love you so much," Jim says, and he kisses me on the lips. I feel that familiar warmth within his kiss, and it's the final indication I need to believe that I am home. I am right where I'm supposed to be.

"My poor eyes! You two get a room already!" my drummer yells in jest.

Jim and I separate, giggling at his silly outburst. We all laugh in unison, and I know that our bond is stronger now than it ever was.

"Group hug!" Jim yells, hugging me softly like I was a fragile, porcelain doll. It feels wonderful being under this type of care. My bandmates, still circled around my bed, all hover over me and hug each other like a human chain.

* * *

This whole experience has transformed me. Life is filled with storms, but also rainbows. Both come and go on their own time. I've learned to love it all because I know that life is special and should always be cherished. We're all special and we all matter. That's not a matter of opinion, that's a fact.

My journey has come full circle, and yet it's a new beginning. I just hope that others can take something from my story and realize that there's always a new path to walk on.

Even though pain comes with every wound, you don't need to hold onto it to heal.

Thank you for reading! If you enjoyed the lyrics to the songs included in the story, you can check out the real songs from my band (Hyper Fury) at

www.hyperfury.com

Made in the USA
Lexington, KY
09 September 2018